MOM'S BIG NEWS

"Are you coming down with something, Mom? They're never going to let us bring the baby home if you have the flu."

"It's not the flu, Cat. And we're not going to adopt." She took a deep breath. "I'm pregnant. You see, there's a new medication that helps women with . . . well, with my problem . . . to have a baby. I've been taking it for about a year. If everything goes according to schedule, you should have a new brother or sister in a little over six months."

I hugged her and tried to keep from jiggling the bed again. "Wow, that's great, Mom. I want to go tell Noreen, okay? This is major news! I can't believe it. I'm going to be a big sister!" I bounded out the back door and jumped on my bike. As I pedaled down the street to Noreen's, my heart practically burst out of my chest with happiness. It didn't occur to me that my life was never going to be the same again.

Other Bantam Skylark Books you will enjoy
Ask your bookseller for the books you have missed

THE AGAINST TAFFY SINCLAIR CLUB by Betsy Haynes
ANASTASIA KRUPNIK by Lois Lowry
ANNE OF GREEN GABLES by L. M. Montgomery
CRY UNCLE! by Mary Jane Auch
DAPHNE'S BOOK by Mary Downing Hahn
THE DOUBLE FUDGE DARE by Louise Ladd
THE GHOST WORE GRAY by Bruce Coville
GOING HOME by Nicholasa Mohr
HORSE CRAZY (The Saddle Club #1) by Bonnie Bryant
JANET HAMM NEEDS A DATE FOR THE DANCE by
    Eve Bunting
MAUD FLIES SOLO by Gibbs Davis
THE ORPHAN GAME by Barbara Cohen
THE SARA SUMMER by Mary Downing Hahn
A WHOLE SUMMER OF WEIRD SUSAN by Louise Ladd

Pick of the Litter

MARY JANE AUCH

A BANTAM SKYLARK BOOK®
NEW YORK · TORONTO · LONDON · SYDNEY · AUCKLAND

Special thanks to Diane Dietz, R.N.

This edition contains the complete text
of the original hardcover edition.
NOT ONE WORD HAS BEEN OMITTED.

PICK OF THE LITTER
A Bantam Skylark Book / published by arrangement with
Holiday House, Inc.

PRINTING HISTORY
Holiday House edition published 1988
Bantam edition / June 1990

ISBN 0-553-15808-2

Published simultaneously in the United States and Canada

Bantam Books are published by Bantam Books, a division of Bantam Doubleday Dell Publishing Group, Inc. Its trademark, consist-
ing of the words "Bantam Books" and the portrayal of a rooster, is
Registered in U.S. Patent and Trademark Office and in other
countries. Marca Registrada. Bantam Books, 666 Fifth Avenue,
New York, New York 10103.

PRINTED IN THE UNITED STATES OF AMERICA

OPM   0 9 8 7 6 5 4 3 2

For KAREN—the "Cat" in our litter

Pick of the Litter

Chapter One

"Not bad," I said to myself, stepping back to admire the results of my morning's work. I had finally arranged my room just the way I wanted it, and the total effect just screamed me, Catherine (better known as Cat) Corwin. It didn't look like your basic eleven-year-old girl's room, either. It was my own special space. My room was pretty big to begin with, but when I pushed the furniture back against the walls, leaving the center of the room open, it was transformed into a dance studio.

I'd been collecting mirrors from various garage sales and the town dump for about a year. Now I had enough to cover one whole wall. I tried out an arabesque and watched my reflection being divided up into segments. I couldn't locate my left leg for a minute, until I adjusted my position and it appeared in the big round mirror with the tarnished gold frame. There were odd-shaped spaces between the mirrors where they didn't quite line up, so the overall effect was more like the fun house at the carnival than the mirrored wall in my teacher's ballet studio, but it served the purpose.

"Cat! Are you in there?" my mother's voice called from the hall.

"Sure, Mom. Come on in." Just before the door opened, it occurred to me that this arrangement wasn't exactly what Mom had had in mind when she "redid" my room last month. The bed with its new spread and dust ruffle were squeezed up against my now mirrorless vanity, wrinkling its matching ruffled skirt, and my dresser was in front of the window, so you could only see the tops of the new curtains.

A look of disbelief crossed Mom's face when she saw the room. "What have you done to this place? Are you moving out?"

"Mom, it's perfect, can't you see? I have the whole middle of the room for dancing now. And look, I even have a mirrored wall."

Mom looked over at my motley collection of mirrors, most of them cracked and one with a long triangular chunk missing from an upper corner. She shook her head. "I hope you aren't superstitious. You must have about seventy-seven years of accumulated bad luck here."

"Broken mirrors are only bad luck to the person who broke them, Mom. Besides it makes a great dance studio. You're not going to make me put it back the way it was, are you?"

"It's your room, Cat. If you don't mind waking up every morning to this, I guess it doesn't bother me." Mom wandered over to the opposite wall to look at my newly arranged poster display. She passed over my collection of ballet and Broadway show posters and stopped to chuckle over a poster-size picture of me and my best friend, Noreen McNulty.

"You and Noreen are about the strangest combination I've ever seen, Cat."

She was right. Noreen and I couldn't have looked less alike if somebody had run all my traits through a computer and asked it to come up with my exact opposite. She was tall and skinny, with a million freckles and fuzzy red hair. I was short and "compact," as my mother put it, with straight dark hair and brown eyes. We met and became best friends in kindergarten. We were still best friends, even though Noreen transferred to the Catholic school in first grade and I stayed in Arnold Avery Elementary.

"Noreen and I may be different on the outside, Mom, but inside we're practically identical twins."

"If you say so," Mom said, sitting down on my bed. She seemed tired, but there was a funny little smile on her face that made me think something was up. I plopped down by my pillow and sat cross-legged, watching her. She looked paler than usual, and there were dark circles under her eyes.

"Are you okay, Mom?" I asked. "You always seem to be tired lately."

"That's just what I wanted to talk about, Cat. There's something important I need to tell you."

My mind started running through the possibilities, like maybe she had some terrible terminal disease or something. Mom cleared her throat and started in. "Do you remember how you used to beg me for a little brother or sister?"

Now this was beginning to feel like the big combination "birds and bees" and "you're old enough now to understand about the fact that you're adopted" lecture she gave me when I was about six.

"Sure. But back then I thought all you had to do was take a cabbage home from the grocery store and you could grow it into a baby."

Mom laughed. "That's right. I'd forgotten about that."

"How could you forget after the scene I made? Remember the time you bought a cabbage and brought it home, then sliced it up for coleslaw? When I went into the kitchen and saw you hacking away at it, I really freaked out."

"That's putting it mildly. It must have taken me an hour to get you calmed down enough so I could understand what all the fuss was about. I still can't imagine where you got that idea in the first place."

"Well, you and Dad always talked about how you chose me to be your daughter. I guess that was your way of working up to the adoption lecture. I put that together with something I heard about babies coming from the cabbage patch, and I figured all the kids in Williamson had started out in the big vegetable display case at the A&P."

"You certainly had an active imagination."

"Well, if you ask me, it made a lot more sense than where babies really come from. *That's* imagination!"

Mom smiled. "I'm sure the idea will appeal to you when you're old enough, Cat. For now, just take my word for it." She picked up my stuffed teddy bear and traced the outline of its ears with her finger. When she looked back at me, I could see little tears glistening in the corners of her eyes. "You remember I told you we adopted you because I wasn't able to have a baby?"

I nodded.

"And you know that we went through years of trying to adopt a second child, and finally it seemed hopeless."

"Sure, Mom," I said. "What are you getting at, anyway?"

She reached over and took my hand. "A wonderful thing has happened, Cat." A tear was moving down her cheek. "You're going to have a baby brother or sister after all."

"Really?" I shouted, bouncing up and down on the bed. "We're going to adopt a baby? Is it a boy or girl? Where is it? When can we pick it up?"

Mom put one hand on my shoulder and the other one over her mouth. "Stop bouncing! You're going to make me lose what little breakfast I managed to get down."

I stopped and reached over to feel her forehead, the way she always did when I was sick. "Are you coming down with something, Mom? They're never going to let us bring the baby home if you have the flu."

"It's not the flu, Cat. And we're not going to adopt." She took a deep breath. "I'm pregnant."

It took a few seconds for her words to sink in. "Really? But how? I mean, I know how . . . but if you never were able to have a baby before, why did it happen now?"

"It didn't just happen. There's a new medication that helps women with . . . well, with my problem . . . to have a baby. I've been taking it for about a year."

"What do you mean? Pills? You told me women took pills so they *wouldn't* have babies."

"These are shots, honey. Anyway, if everything goes according to schedule, you should have a new brother or sister in a little over six months. Sometime around the end of August."

I hugged her and tried to keep from jiggling the

bed again. "Wow, that's great, Mom. I want to go tell Noreen, okay? This is major news!"

"Sure, Cat. Now that everything seems to be progressing normally, I guess it's all right to spread the word."

"Thanks, Mom," I yelled as I ran down the stairs. "I can't believe it. I'm going to be a big sister!" I bounded out the back door and jumped on my bike. As I pedaled down the street to Noreen's, my heart practically burst out of my chest with happiness. It didn't occur to me that my life was never going to be the same again.

Chapter Two

The McNultys' house always had a dozen kids spilling in and out of it, and at least half of them lived there. Noreen was the only girl in a family of six children. I parked my bike by the front porch, stepped over a tricycle, two Big Wheels, and a beat-up old football, and knocked on the door. Four kids—only two, Billy and Ryan, were McNultys—had begun the annual Monopoly game on the front porch and were arguing over it already. The McNultys made up the rules as they went along and could keep a single Monopoly game going for months, starting with the first warm day in spring and stretching through to Labor Day.

I could see Noreen back in the kitchen, trying to stuff some sloppy-looking purple goop into Patrick, the baby. Mike and Danny, older than Patrick but younger than Billy and Ryan, were fighting on the living room couch and had the TV turned up to hyper-loud. I had to bang on the door and yell a few times before Noreen looked up and motioned for me to come in.

"Hi, Cat. I can't do anything until I get Patrick fed. It might take a while. He's being a beast. Have a seat."

I looked around for a place to sit, but every flat surface was covered with old newspapers, dirty dishes, and piles of clean, sorted laundry.

"I've got terrific news, Noreen. Absolutely wonderful, stupendous news."

"Really?" She looked away from Patrick for a second with the goop-laden spoon poised in midair over the high-chair tray. "What is it? Tell me. . . . Aw, Patrick!"

Patrick had pulled down on the spoon and let go suddenly, turning it into a slingshot that whapped a diagonal purple stripe across the front of Noreen's yellow shirt.

"Yuck! What is that stuff?" I asked, moving out of Patrick's range.

Noreen wiped off her shirt with a dark blue sock from one of the laundry piles, then carefully folded it and put it back with its mate. "I don't know. Prunes, or maybe beets."

"How can you feed the poor kid something if you don't even know what it is?"

Noreen loaded up the spoon again. "What difference does it make? Patrick doesn't care. He thinks of food as ammunition."

Patrick had clamped his mouth shut in a determined grin, and Noreen was scraping the spoon back and forth across his lips, trying to squeeze some goop through the crack.

"So tell me your news," Noreen said, keeping her eye on Patrick this time.

"Well, you're not going to believe this, but my mom just told me that she's . . ."

I was interrupted by the slamming of the screen door and a lot of yelling.

"Noreen, Ryan just bought a hotel for Park Place after I already landed on it, and now he wants to charge me more rent. That's cheating, isn't it?"

"Is not! Billy's still there, so he pays. Right, Nor?"

"You can't do that! Cheater, cheater, lizard eater!"

Noreen handed me the spoon. "Here, feed the beast for a minute, will you? I have to go be referee." She collared the two kids and headed them back to the porch.

Patrick was just sitting there grinning at me. I spooned up some of the purple stuff and held it out to him. He opened his mouth without an argument and let me feed him. With the next spoonful, he practically met me halfway. By the time Noreen got back into the room, Patrick's dish was almost empty. Taking care of babies was a cinch. I was going to make one terrific big sister.

"I don't know why you make such a big deal about feeding Patrick, Noreen. He's been a little angel with me." I turned to give Noreen my superior look.

"An angel? Patrick? I don't think he's... Watch out, Cat!"

Before I could turn back, I could feel something warm and wet sliding down the side of my face.

"Sorry," Noreen said, handing me a dark green sock. "I thought you knew. Patrick stores stuff in his cheeks and then lets loose when you're not looking. You gotta make sure he swallows each time."

"How's a person supposed to know something like that?" I grumbled, wiping the goop off my face. "I hate to be the one to break the news to you, but I think your baby brother's a mental case."

"Hear that, Patrick?" Noreen asked, mopping up Patrick's tray and face with one swoop. "Cat thinks you're bananas." She made a face at him, and he giggled as she picked him up. "He's not going to eat anything else, so I'll take him out on the porch, and the boys can watch him. Come on."

Noreen had spoken too loudly. There was a sudden scraping of chairs, and the last of the McNultys dived over the porch railing just as we got to the screen door. A bright orange five-hundred-dollar bill hung suspended above the table for a second, then seesawed its way down to land in the front bushes.

"Darn you kids!" Noreen yelled, shifting Patrick to her other hip. "I'm telling Ma."

"Does this mean you're going to have to take care of him all afternoon?" I asked.

"Not if I can help it. He can watch TV with Mike and Danny."

Unfortunately, Noreen had a voice that could be heard over a rock concert. You had to have that kind of voice to survive in her house. So by the time we got back into the living room, the TV was still on, but nobody was watching it.

"Rats! They're getting faster every day." Noreen stomped over to the cellar door and opened it. "Ma! The boys all took off and left me with Patrick again."

Mrs. McNulty struggled upstairs with another load of laundry and dumped it on the couch. Then she sat down next to the pile of clothes and reached out for Patrick. Mrs. McNulty was a padded version of Noreen, with no sharp corners sticking out to poke into her kids when she hugged them. "What's the matter, Pumpkin?" she said to Patrick. "Everybody running out on you today?"

"The boys should take their turn now, Ma. I folded the laundry and fed Patrick," Noreen said.

Patrick squirmed out of Noreen's arms and burrowed into his mother's lap, happily rubbing his forehead back and forth against her shoulder. "Go ahead,

Noreen. You've done enough for this morning. I'll watch him."

"That's not the point, Ma. The boys always run off and get away with it."

Mrs. McNulty smiled as she nuzzled Patrick's fuzz of reddish-blond hair. "Boys will be boys, Noreen. They're not so good at caring for babies as we women are. That's the way it's meant to be. Go ahead and play now. Just be back in time to set the table for supper."

Noreen stormed out of the house. I followed, narrowly missing getting smashed in the face by the door.

"Wait up!" I yelled, breaking into a trot to catch up. "What are you so mad about? Your mother let you go, didn't she?"

When Noreen got mad, her cheeks turned bright red, fusing all of her freckles into two big blobs. "Oh sure, she let me go. After I worked the whole morning and the boys just watched TV and played games. That's great! That's just terrific!"

"Well, at least you're free for the afternoon. Wait till you hear my news." I thought maybe that would get her attention, but I couldn't even slow her down.

"Boys will be boys," she mimicked. "We women are better at caring for babies. Baloney! It doesn't take any talent to wipe a runny nose."

"Listen," I said. "I've got to tell you . . ."

"And did you hear the part about being back in time to set the table? Just because Mike and Danny are total morons doesn't mean they can't manage to put out a few forks and spoons. So what was your news, anyway?"

"Mom just told me this morning. You're not going to believe it."

"Believe what? Come on. Out with it."

"Well . . ." I said, drawing out the suspense, now that I had her attention. "Sometime around the end of August, there's going to be a big event in our family."

Noreen cracked her gum. "Am I going to hear this news, or what? So what's the big event?"

"My mother's going to have a baby."

That stopped Noreen. "Oh, Cat. No!"

"What do you mean? It's great. I'm finally going to be a big sister, just like you."

Noreen stood with her hands on her hips, nodding. "That's what I meant. You know what I go through all the time."

This wasn't the reaction I'd expected. "This is different. I'm really excited about the baby. I've always wanted a brother or sister. How much trouble can one little baby be?"

"One baby isn't so bad, Cat. It's just that there's always another and another, and pretty soon you're living in a zoo."

"My mother isn't going to have any other babies. She had to take shots to get this one."

Noreen laughed. "Were you sleeping all year in health class? Women don't get pregnant from having shots. They get pregnant from . . ."

"I know, I know. . . . They did it the regular way. The shots just help or something. Anyway, the least you can do, as my very best friend in the whole world, is be excited for me. I can't wait for the baby to be born. Honest."

Noreen started walking again. "Okay. I'm sorry, Cat. It's just that I've always envied you for being an only child. You get all the attention, and you have that big room and everything."

"What do you think my mother's giving birth to—a brontosaurus? I'll still have my room. Mom's turning her little sewing room into a nursery. Nothing's going to change for me."

Noreen bit her lip. "Yeah, I guess you're right. One little baby isn't going to make all that much difference."

Chapter Three

A couple of weeks later Noreen came over to our house to get a ride to ballet class. We were already in the car when Mom came out. She eased herself into the car, trying to squeeze behind the steering wheel. "Watch out, kids. I'm going to move this seat back a bit." The seat lurched back four or five notches, and I looked over to see if Mom's feet still reached the pedals. They did—barely.

"If you move back any further, Mom, you'll be a backseat driver," I said.

"Cars must be designed by men," Mom grumbled. "They certainly don't have pregnant women in mind." Her driving was a little jumpier than usual, but she managed to get us downtown to Madame Yvette's dance studio.

"Wow," Noreen said as Mom drove off. "Are you sure your mother isn't giving birth to a brontosaurus after all?"

"What's that supposed to mean?" I asked.

"Well, she's getting so big."

"Don't be dumb, Noreen. All pregnant women get big."

"Not *that* big, that fast. I've gone through five babies with my mother, and by the time she looked like your mother, she had her suitcase packed to go to the hospital. Your mother isn't due for over five months yet."

"Well, people are different, that's all." Actually, I'd been kind of wondering about that myself. Soon after Mom told me about the baby, she started blowing up like a balloon.

We were the first ones in the dressing room, and we piled our stuff on a couple of chairs in the corner. "I just had a terrible thought," Noreen said, slipping out of her jeans.

"What?"

"Maybe your mother's going to have twins. Would that be a disaster, or what?"

"She's not going to have twins."

"How do you know?"

"Because twins run in families. Nobody in our family ever had twins, so forget it." I heard a shrill voice coming from down the hall. "Let's get out of here. That's Wella Mae Riddle." We finished changing and ran into the studio just in time to avoid her.

Noreen and I each picked our favorite spot at the

barre and started with plié in first position. I watched our two reflections in the mirrors. Everything Noreen did looked so graceful and easy. She was a natural.

That's what Madame Yvette had said the first time she saw Noreen dance. I'd already been studying ballet a whole year when I took Noreen along on Bring-a-Friend Day. Dad said it was just Madame's way of suckering new kids into taking expensive lessons, but it didn't work that way for Noreen. When Madame found out that the McNultys didn't have any money for extras like ballet, she gave Noreen a full scholarship.

A couple of kids arrived and took spots near the other end of the barre. "I wonder who'll be getting solos in this year's recital?" Noreen whispered.

"Three guesses. You, of course, and probably that obnoxious Wella Mae Riddle."

"Well, maybe you will too, Cat."

"Oh sure. If everybody else drops dead before the recital."

"No, really. You're doing much better this year, especially now that you have your own studio to practice in every day."

We worked through the warm-ups in silence. Noreen's leg lifted up as if it were attached to a pulley from the ceiling. Mine looked as if it had lead weights hanging from it.

Noreen was watching our reflections, too. "Push a little higher, Cat. An extra inch or two of lift makes a big difference."

"An extra six inches of leg makes a big difference, too," I grumbled. "Your leg is higher up than mine to begin with. No wonder it looks so easy when you do it."

The studio was filling up fast now. Wella Mae Riddle came in wearing a turquoise leotard, about the fourteenth new one she'd had this year. She slipped into the spot next to me. "I can't wait until Madame announces the solos for the recital, can you, Cat? The suspense is just killing me."

I caught Noreen's eye in the mirror, and she made a face. "Yeah, Wella Mae. It's killing me too," I said.

Wella Mae started warming up and pretended to be looking off in space, but I could tell she was watching her reflection in the mirrors on the other side of the room. "I'm so nervous," Wella Mae whined. "Madame said she'd make the announcements at the beginning of class today, and I just know I won't make it this year. I have this awful feeling that I just didn't do well enough in class last week. That's when Madame was deciding, you know. I could tell by the way she was watching us, making mental notes. And I really goofed in the pirouettes—only a wobbly double instead of my usual perfect triple. I just know I didn't . . ."

"Knock it off, Wella Mae," Noreen said. "You know darn well you have a solo, so don't be cute."

Just then Madame Yvette strode into the room and tapped her walking stick to quiet us. Madame always looked as if she were making an entrance on stage. Her steps were long and smooth, so her head stayed at the same level when she walked instead of bouncing up and down like an ordinary person's. Madame perched on the tall stool she used during class and set down the walking stick. She pulled a folded piece of paper out of her pocket. "I'm sure you're anxious to hear about the recital dances, so if you'll gather around me, I'll give you the news."

Everyone settled in at her feet. Wella Mae was right in front, of course. Madame started off with the group dances. The first one, a rainbow dance, would have everybody in the class in it. Noreen and I both got called as "greens"—my least favorite color in the whole world. Lucky Wella Mae got to be a lavender. Then Madame announced that each color would have a soloist. Naturally, Noreen was the head green. And guess who was the big-shot lavender?

Madame reeled off the names for a few more dances, mostly groups of six or eight. Then she called my name to be in the Dance of the Four Swans from *Swan Lake* with three other girls. This was the first time I'd ever been singled out for a small group. Noreen poked me with her foot and grinned.

"Three girls have been chosen for solos this year," Madame continued. They are Margo Vinetti, Noreen McNulty, and Wella Mae Riddle." Noreen just smiled and looked embarrassed, but Wella Mae was making a big deal about how relieved she was, fanning herself with her hand and rolling her eyes.

"And for our grand finale we're going to have a circus dance, with a ringmaster, acrobats, trapeze artists, clowns, and circus ponies. Although you all will be in this number, there will be two featured dancers —Noreen McNulty as the trainer of the circus ponies, and Wella Mae Riddle as the ringmaster." Wella Mae put on her big surprised act while Madame kept talking. "Since these are very important roles, we need to have understudies. These girls will learn the solos so that they can step in, in case of an emergency at recital time. Understudy for Noreen is Margo Vinetti, and understudy for Wella Mae will be Catherine Corwin."

Me? I couldn't believe it! I was dying to talk to Noreen, but Madame picked up her stick and started beating time with it to start the first barre exercise. She had fits if any of us talked during class. By the time class was over, I was about ready to burst.

Noreen hugged me. "Didn't I tell you you were doing better this year? Congratulations."

"Yeah, thanks. You too," I said. "But you getting a

solo didn't come as a surprise. Me being an understudy is a shock."

Wella Mae walked up to us. She had dropped the modest act by now and was just being her usual obnoxious self. "Don't work yourself up into a frenzy trying to learn the ringmaster part, Cat. I haven't been sick a day since kindergarten, and I don't intend to start now. Anyway, if the part is designed to show off my abilities as a dancer, I really don't see how you could even begin to learn it."

"Buzz off, Wella Mae," Noreen said. "Madame Yvette is the one who decides who can do what around here, not you."

Dad was waiting in the car when we got out.

"Hi, Dad. What happened to Mom?" I asked, as Noreen and I climbed into the back seat.

"Driving is getting pretty difficult for your mother, Cat. When she gets the seat back far enough to fit behind the steering wheel, she's practically driving with the tips of her toes."

"Yeah, I noticed," I said. "Dad, you'll never guess what. I'm Wella Mae Riddle's understudy for one of the leads in the big finale."

"No kidding? That's great, Cat. All your hard work must be paying off."

"I know. The only problem is that Wella Mae says she never gets sick, so my chances of performing in the recital are pretty slim."

"Cat's right, Mr. Corwin," Noreen said. "Wella Mae has been in my class since first grade, and she always gets the perfect attendance award at the end of the year. She might get a little sniffle once in a while, but she comes to school anyway. Then everybody else gets sick, and she's fine."

"So she's the 'Typhoid Mary' of St. Agnes Elementary?" Dad asked.

"You got it," Noreen said. "Wella Mae is indestructible."

"That makes sense," Dad said. "It's probably where she gets her name from."

"What do you mean?" I asked.

"Wella Mae, get it?" Dad persisted.

Noreen and I just looked at each other. Neither of us got it.

Dad caught my eye in the rearview mirror. "Well-a Mae instead of Sick-a Mae?"

Noreen and I both groaned. We were used to Dad's corny puns, but he faked us out every time.

"Forget the jokes, Dad," I said. "I have a serious problem here."

"You could always resort to germ warfare," Dad suggested.

Noreen poked me. "We could have Wella Mae baby-sit for Patrick. He catches every bug that comes around."

We pulled up in front of Noreen's house and

dropped her off. "Thanks for the ride, Mr. Corwin. See you tomorrow, Cat."

"Yeah," I said. "Let me know if you have any more bright ideas about how to get rid of Sick-a Mae." I climbed over into the front with Dad and almost sat on a package that was next to him on the seat.

"What's this?" I asked, picking it up.

"Just something for the baby."

I looked inside. "A Nerf football? Isn't it a little early to be thinking about playing ball with the kid?"

"Well, it's soft. I thought the baby might like it. It'll get him used to the idea of playing football when he's older."

"Him?"

"Or her," Dad said, pulling into our driveway. "Girls can play football, too, you know."

"Not this girl. I'm terrible at everything we do in gym except square dancing."

"I know. You're strictly the sugar-and-spice-and-everything-nice type. A throwback to the fifties."

I reached out and stopped Dad as he was about to get out of the car. "Dad? Did you ever wish I was a boy?"

"Of course not. Where did you ever get that idea?"

"Well, if the baby's a boy, are you going to like him better than me?"

"Get that nonsense out of your head, Cat. A father loves all of his kids. Maybe he loves them for different reasons, but he loves them equally. Now let's get inside. Your mother probably has dinner ready."

When we went into the kitchen, dinner was just barely started. "Hey, Mom," I said. "Guess what? I'm Wella Mae's understudy for the ringmaster in the big circus dance."

"That's great, Cat."

"Only Wella Mae never gets sick, so I don't think my chances of performing it are that..." I suddenly realized that nobody was listening to me. Dad had handed Mom the package with the football in it. When she opened it, the two of them got all giggly, like a couple of lovesick teenagers.

I raised my voice. "But it doesn't really matter because there was this Hollywood agent visiting class today, and he said he wants me to star in his next movie. Isn't that great?"

Mom glanced up and smiled. "That's wonderful, honey. Walter, I want you to come upstairs and see what I've done with the baby's room. I'm having so much fun. . . ."

Her voice faded as the two of them went upstairs. I walked out to the backyard. I wasn't excited about the recital anymore. What difference did it make? Nobody cared about it anyway.

I was aimlessly wandering around when I heard something in the bushes. A skinny gray cat appeared, looking hungry and frightened. He was about halfway across the yard when he spotted me and stopped dead.

"Here, kitty," I called. "Come over here. I won't hurt you."

The cat stayed motionless until I got up. Then he darted for the bushes and disappeared.

Without the distraction of the cat, I started thinking about the baby again and the changes it would make in my life. I remembered what Dad had said in the car—a father loves all of his kids. Then I thought about the way the two of them got so silly over the stupid toy for the baby and weren't even interested in my dance recital. The trouble was, I wasn't really their kid. Not the same way the baby would be.

Chapter Four

"You have the best room of any kid I know," Noreen said.

We'd been practicing the recital dances in my room every day for almost two weeks. She was running through the last part of her solo, and I had to keep my finger on the arm of the stereo because there was a big scratch in the record, and it kept skipping.

"It's so great to have space to practice," Noreen said. "The only place at my house where there's any privacy and a mirror is the bathroom. It's rather limiting."

It always amazed me the way Noreen could talk and dance at the same time. I couldn't do that because I was always too busy saying "one-and-two-and-three" under my breath. I moved my finger by mistake, and the record jumped. Noreen paused, then figured out where she was supposed to be and caught up. She did the last series of spins diagonally across the room and hit her final position without even looking dizzy.

Every time I tried those turns, my eyes crossed for the next five minutes, and I staggered around like a wino. Madame said it was because I didn't "spot."

Noreen flopped down on my bed. "Okay, Cat. Your turn. Do you want to practice *Swan Lake* or the ring-master?"

"We'd better do the *Swan Lake* thing. I still can't do it on the right beat."

In the Swan Dance, Madame had the four of us lined up side by side, holding hands with our arms crossed in front. It was hard enough just getting the position right, but as soon as we started moving, it was a disaster. There were a lot of small bouncy steps, and the other three girls, Alison, Kim, and Cara, stayed exactly in time with each other. For some reason I always started too soon or too late. When everybody else was up on pointe, I was down on flat feet, and by the time I got up, they were down. The other problem was that we moved sideways across the stage, then switched direction and went back, but I never switched at the same time. While they were zagging, I was still zigging.

"Come on," Noreen said. "Starting position."

"It's not the same with just one other person, Noreen. When we do it in class, I'm outnumbered."

"Don't worry. I had the same problem when I did

this dance a couple of years ago, but everything finally fell into place. Remember, I had to do it with Wella Mae, which was even worse."

"Yeah. At least Alison, Kim, and Cara are nice. I guess I should be thankful for that."

We got into the starting position and shifted around until we could see ourselves in a couple of the mirrors. What a team! I only came up to Noreen's chin, and her bony elbow stuck into my shoulder.

Noreen started counting and practically yanked my arm off when she started and I didn't.

"You could give a person some warning before you take off," I said.

"Sorry. I'll give you four counts before we begin again. Make sure you take the first step on 'one.'"

We had three more false starts, and then I finally got it right. "You're doing it, Cat," Noreen shouted. "Isn't this fun?"

"Three-and . . . yeah, great . . . four-and-five-and . . ." I was lost.

"There's no 'five-and,' Cat. Just four beats. Let's start over."

This time I didn't try to talk, and we made it through the whole thing.

"What did I tell you?" Noreen whooped. "It's a cinch, right?"

I didn't have to give her an honest answer because there was a knock on the door, and Mom came in. At least her stomach came in; then she followed. She had a funny expression on her face.

"Hi, Mrs. Corwin," Noreen said. "Want to see Cat and me do her *Swan Lake* dance? She's really got it."

"Oh, that's nice. But not right now, Noreen. First I have some news." She looked at me.

"You want me to leave, Mrs. Corwin?"

Mom eased herself down on the bed. "No, of course not, Noreen. I'm sure Cat would want to share our news with you anyway."

Noreen and I sat on the floor in front of her. "What's up, Mom?"

"Well, your father just took me for my doctor's appointment, and it seems we're not going to have a baby after all."

Noreen gave me a look. The vision of a brontosaurus flashed through my mind.

"Just what *are* we having, Mom?" I asked warily.

Mom grinned. "Dr. Braxton was almost positive he heard two heartbeats. He said he suspected I might be carrying more than one baby, because I'm larger than I should be for four months. I have to go to the hospital next week for a sonogram."

"A what?" I asked, ignoring Noreen's elbow pushing subtly into my ribs.

"A sonogram. That's when they take a picture of babies before they're born. Then we'll know for sure if we're going to have twins."

I got up and hugged her. "Twins. That's terrific, Mom. Nobody in my whole school has twins in the family."

"Mine either," Noreen said. She gave me another look.

"Well, I'll let you two get back to your practicing. I just couldn't wait to tell you the news."

As soon as the door was closed, Noreen started in on me. "Ha! Did I or did I not tell you your mother was having twins?"

"We don't know that for sure yet. Besides, what would be so bad about twins? They might be kind of fun."

"How much time are your parents going to have for you when they have two little babies to worry about? And who do you think is going to have to pitch in every time the work gets out of hand?"

"You just can't judge everybody else's family by your own, Noreen. You have five brothers. I'm only getting twin babies."

Noreen got a wicked grin on her face. "I want you to picture something in your mind, Cat."

"Picture what?"

"Two Patricks."

I could picture it, all right. Maybe a brontosaurus wouldn't have been so bad after all!

ChapterFive

The day Mom had her appointment for the sonogram, we all went along. Dad had to get off work, and Mom let me stay home from school because she said it would be "an educational experience."

I'd never been in a hospital before. "This place is huge," I said. "I didn't think there were this many sick people in the whole city."

"They're not all sick, Cat," Mom said. "A lot of people are coming here for tests, like me."

We found the X-ray department and sat in the waiting room until a lady in a white coat with a name-tag that said Ms. Pitzerose came out to talk to Mom.

"I'd like my husband and daughter to see the sonogram if they could," Mom said.

"That will be fine, Mrs. Corwin. We'll get you set up first, and we'll call them in later." She took Mom into a dark-looking room while Dad and I stayed in the waiting room.

"Do you think this sonogram thing is going to hurt, Dad?"

"No. I'm sure it's painless, just like an X ray."

"Then why do you look worried?"

"I'm not worried, Cat. I was just thinking about what it will mean if we have twins. We'll have to get two of everything. We hadn't counted on that."

"Oh." I could tell Dad was worried about how expensive it would be. He always got the same look on his face when he spread all the bills out on the kitchen table every month.

Pretty soon Ms. Pitzerose came to the door. "Mr. Corwin, would you come in now, please?" I started to get up too, but she said, "Maybe your daughter should wait a few minutes." Then she looked at me. "I'll come back out for you, honey." I hate it when strangers call me "honey."

It seemed as if they were in there forever. I thumbed through an old issue of *People* magazine to keep my mind occupied. What was taking so long? Something must be wrong, or they would have let me right in. Maybe it was a brontosaurus after all. They probably had double heartbeats or something. I'd be the first kid in Arnold Avery Elementary to have a brontosaurus as a baby brother. I'd be the first kid in the whole world to have one! I held up the *People* magazine and imagined a picture of myself on the cover changing a diaper on a baby dinosaur.

"You can come in now, Cat. We have a surprise for you." Ms. Pitzerose was smiling.

She led me into the dark room. It was divided up by curtains, and she pulled one aside and let me into a cubicle. Dad was there, and Mom was lying on a table, all covered up with a sheet except for her bare stomach, which looked like a huge pink beach ball with a belly button. This was really embarrassing.

Mom and Dad were both grinning like fools, and Mom reached over and took my hand. "Watch the TV screen over there, Cat. Ms. Pitzerose will show you something."

There was this big machine with a round black-and-white TV screen on top, but I couldn't make out what the picture was. I thought a fancy hospital like this ought to be able to afford a color TV, but I didn't say anything. Then Ms. Pitzerose started moving a paddle-shaped thing around on Mom's stomach, and the picture changed.

"Watch closely, Cat," Ms. Pitzerose said. "There. That's the first one. Can you see it?" She reached over to the TV with her other hand and traced a pale circle with her finger.

"The first what? What am I supposed to see?"

"That's a baby's head," Mom said.

It just looked like a blob to me, but everybody was getting pretty worked up about it.

Ms. Pitzerose was on the move again with her paddle. "Look. There's number two. And..." Her voice was getting higher and squeakier by the minute. "There's the third head. Isn't this exciting?"

I couldn't believe it. "We're having a three-headed baby?" I blurted out.

Everybody started laughing, and I thought they'd all gone nuts.

Mom squeezed my hand. "No, Cat. Three babies. Triplets!"

I pulled my hand away and walked over to the screen. It still looked like just a bunch of shadows to me, and they were jiggling now because Mom was still laughing.

Ms. Pitzerose moved the paddle around and pointed out some more things to me. "Look, Cat. Here's an arm and a body and two legs."

"Oh yeah. Now I see it. There's another pair of legs over there. They're so small, though."

Mom beamed. "Well, they aren't due to be born for almost another five months. They'll grow a lot before then."

Ms. Pitzerose looked at her watch. "Yes, they certainly will. Now, Cat, if you'll take your father back to the waiting room, we'll finish up."

In the waiting room I realized Dad hadn't said anything the whole time we'd been in with Mom. He finally spoke up. "So... triplets! Kind of a surprise ...huh, Cat?"

"That's putting it mildly," I said.

"Can't get over it," Dad said. "Three of them."

He sat there grinning and shaking his head until Mom came out. "Here's a present for you, Cat," Mom said. She handed me a dark picture.

"What is it?" I asked, turning the picture around a couple of times. "It looks like the TV screen, but I can't figure out where anything is."

"It shows all three babies. See?"

Mom traced the heads with her finger; then I could see them. "Yeah, Mom. Thanks." I stuffed the picture into my jacket pocket.

Noreen was right. You start with one little baby, and next thing you know, you're living in a zoo. I decided right then that I wouldn't tell her about the triplets. She'd made such a big deal about twins, she'd really go off the deep end if she knew Mom was having three babies. Besides, I didn't want to think about the triplets myself until they arrived. Maybe if we all forgot about them, they'd go away.

I managed to keep my secret for a whole month. It wasn't so hard because I just pretended I never heard about the triplets. Each time Mom or Dad started talking about them, which was about every other minute, I'd leave the room or start humming to myself so I couldn't hear. Noreen finally got used to the idea of twins and stopped bugging me about that. Besides, we were really busy getting ready for the recital, so we had other things to talk about.

Then one day something happened, and I couldn't ignore the problem of the triplets any longer. Mom and Dad and I went to McDonald's for supper one night. Mom wasn't cooking much these days because her stomach wouldn't let her get close enough to the stove. The only problem was that it wouldn't let her fit into the booth at McDonald's either. Dad trailed after her with a tray of Big Macs, milkshakes, and fries while she tried a couple more booths. Being out in public with a mother who looked like a human weather balloon was extremely embarrassing. She finally gave up and sat sideways at one of those little tables, and Dad and I sat at the next one. "Diane, I was just thinking," Dad said as he took the stuff off the tray and slid it over to her table. "Do you realize you're carrying around over half of a basketball team?"

"Believe me, I realize it, Walter," Mom said, resting her hands on her stomach. "I think there may be a basketball game going on in here as we speak."

When most babies move, you have to put your hand on the mother's stomach to feel them. Mom was so big that when our babies moved you could *see* them right through her clothes.

"People are looking," I whispered. Darcy Stepanowski, a girl in my class, was sitting at another table with her family. They were all staring at my mother with their mouths hanging open.

"Cat, this isn't something I can stop and start at will. Whenever I sit down, the babies have to wiggle around to find a comfortable spot. They'll settle down in a minute. Remember, there are three of them in there. It's a bit cramped."

I opened my Big Mac and tried to change the subject. "Madame Yvette says I'm doing much better this year. I told her about my dance studio at home, and she says that's why. She says if I keep practicing every day, I should have my own solo by next year."

Mom had to unwrap her Big Mac with one hand because her other hand wouldn't reach all the way around her stomach. "Cat, you're getting pretty grown up now, and I think you can understand the changes that these three babies are going to make in our lives. This isn't going to be the same as bringing home one baby."

"Yeah, Mom. I know."

Mom wiped off some of the Big Mac juice that had dribbled down her front. "Your father and I have been talking about how we'll have to do some rearranging in the house—change some of the rooms around upstairs."

"Change *which* rooms around upstairs. Not mine."

Mom shot a look at Dad, and he cleared his throat but didn't say anything.

"You're not messing with *my* room, are you?"

"I know how much that dance studio means to you, honey," Mom said, "but my sewing room isn't going to be big enough for the babies now. Your father and I have measured it, and there's just no way it will work for triplets. We're going to need space for three bassinets and a changing table, plus all the diapers and dressers for the baby clothes and . . ."

"You're giving the babies *my* room?"

"I'm afraid we don't have any choice, Cat," Dad said. "Maybe if we can get some money saved up, we can build an extra room onto the house someday, but there's no time for that before the babies come."

"Wait a minute. This is only the middle of May. You said the babies weren't due until the end of August. Can't I at least have my room until then?"

Mom had been sipping her milkshake from a straw and had the cup resting on her stomach, like it was a shelf. The Stepanowskis were taking that all in, too. "That was when we thought there was only one baby. When you're having triplets, there's a good chance they might be born early. We need to get ready for them right now."

I took another bite of my Big Mac, but my throat knotted up when I tried to swallow. I put it back in the box and closed it.

"Aren't you going to finish that?" Mom asked.

"I'm not hungry. I'll save it for later."

"I hope you're not upset about the room, Cat," Dad said.

"No problem, Dad." I could feel the tears starting. Darcy was still staring at us, and I didn't want to cry in the middle of McDonald's, so I grabbed my Big Mac and got up. "It's hot in here. I'll wait for you guys in the car."

I bawled my eyes out in the backseat, but I was finished by the time Mom and Dad came out. Nobody said much on the way home. As soon as we got in the house, Mom and Dad went upstairs to start making plans for my room. Now I had to tell Noreen. Things had gone too far, and I needed to talk to her. I called her house, but Ryan said she was over at their cousin's and wouldn't be home until late.

I went out on the back steps to think. I was sitting there, feeling sorry for myself, when something hairy brushed against my leg. As I jumped up, the gray cat ran toward the bushes. He tried to drag my Big Mac box with him but dropped it about halfway across the yard.

"Here, kitty, kitty." He stuck his head out from under the bush, and I could tell he really wanted the food but didn't quite have the guts to come get it. I went over and sat on the grass where he had dropped the box. I opened it and pulled off a little piece of the meat.

"Come here, boy. You want some of this?" I tossed

it close to his hiding spot. He sniffed the air and moved out from the bush. He was so thin, you could see his ribs and all the little bumpy bones down his back. He crept toward the piece of meat, never taking his eyes off me. Then he grabbed it and darted for cover again.

He tilted his head first to one side, then the other, as he chewed. He downed it in one big lumpy swallow and stared at me, licking his face to taste the last few traces of meat juice. I tossed one piece of meat after another, throwing shorter and shorter distances, so he had to keep coming closer. Each time he went through the same thing, always running back to the safety of the bush and watching me with huge green eyes as he ate. Finally he came close enough for me to touch him, and I reached out, but he ran off and disappeared. I went back up on the steps and waited quietly, leaving the rest of the meat and the roll out in the yard, but the cat was gone for good.

I shoved my hands into my jacket pockets and felt a folded piece of stiff paper. When I took it out, I realized it was the picture of the sonogram. I'd forgotten it was in there. I smoothed out the creases and looked at it more closely.

The babies were lurking in shadows, like creepy little goblins. They were taking my room away already. What would they take away from me after they were born?

Chapter Six

The next day after school, I was in my room taking down my posters, when I heard the doorbell ring, then footsteps charging up the stairs. "Hey, Cat! I've got great news." It was Noreen. "I can only stay a minute because I have to watch the kids while Mom goes grocery shopping, but I couldn't wait to tell...." She came into my room and stopped dead when she saw all of the cartons in the middle of the floor. "Hey, what's going on? It looks like you're moving."

"I am," I said, feeling the tears start again.

Noreen sat down on my bed. "You're kidding. You can't move now. It'll ruin everything. Where are you going?"

"Just across the hall," I mumbled.

Noreen brightened. "You mean your mom's letting you put your bed and stuff into her sewing room so this room can be just for dancing? Cat Corwin, you are the luckiest kid I know."

"Sure, Noreen. I'm going to have two rooms, and we're putting the babies on the roof."

Noreen slumped back on the pillow. "Darn. I forgot about the babies."

"I wish I could," I said, going over to close the door. "You won't believe what's happened now." I started to cry.

Noreen's eyes got wide. "What's the matter? They're not giving your room to the babies, are they?"

I nodded.

Noreen looked around the room. "That's dumb. Two little babies don't need all this space."

"No, but three little babies do."

"Three? Triplets?"

It nodded.

"Wait a minute. How do you know that?"

"The test Mom had last month, the sonogram. They could tell."

Noreen choked and almost swallowed her bubble gum. "Three babies in one shot. That's too awful to even think about."

I blew my nose. "Thanks, Noreen. I knew you'd think of something comforting to say."

Noreen's eyes narrowed. "Wait a minute. You told me the sonogram just showed twins. You lied to me."

"I didn't say that. You said, 'The sonogram showed your mother's having more than one baby, didn't it?'

and I just said yes. I never said how many more than one baby she was having, so that's not lying."

"It may not be exactly lying, but it's sneaky, Cat Corwin. Why didn't you tell me? We're supposed to be best friends."

"Sure. Some friend you are. You've been the voice of gloom ever since I told you about the first baby. Then you were so upset about the twins, I figured triplets would freak you out completely. Anyway, I just didn't want to talk about it. So, what's your great news? Maybe it'll cheer me up."

"You bet it will. It's Wella Mae. She was showing off on the playground at recess. We have one of those merry-go-round things. You know—a platform with handles and a bunch of kids run around to get it going, then everybody jumps on and then..."

"I know! I know! So what happened to Wella Mae?"

Noreen gave me one of her looks and blew a bubble. She loved to tell long stories and hated to be rushed.

She popped the bubble and pushed the gum back into her mouth with her finger. "Well, she got up on the platform when nobody else was on it and yelled, 'Look, everybody. I'm on stage.' Then she started doing pirouettes—triples. Sister Mary Ignatius just about had a bird because every time Wella Mae spun around, her pleated uniform skirt flew up and you could see her underpants—Wella Mae's, not Sister's."

Noreen paused and blew another bubble, waiting for me to interrupt, but I didn't. "So anyway, half the boys in the school were crowding around the merry-go-round, and Wella Mae kept pirouetting, and Sister Mary Ignatius was swooping across the playground like the Wicked Witch of the West...when it happened." She paused again and grinned, stretching the gum into a long string.

I couldn't stand it. "*What* happened?" I yelled.

Noreen poked the gum back into her mouth and cracked it a few times. "Well, Sister was pushing her way through the crowd of boys when she tripped. I don't think anybody tripped her on purpose, but you never can tell about some of those kids. Anyway, Sister reached out to grab the handle of the merry-go-round to catch herself, and when she did, the whole thing started to move. Wella Mae was in mid-pirouette, and she fell sideways. She did a double flip over one of the handles and landed on top of Gino Vivino."

"Was she hurt?"

"Broken arm," Noreen said. "Your ticket to stardom!"

"Aw, be serious, Noreen. It'll take more than a broken arm to keep Wella Mae out of that recital. Two broken legs, maybe, but not a stupid arm. She'll still show up."

"Not in traction, she won't."

"Traction? You're kidding."

"Nope. She broke it in four places. Won't be out of the hospital for at least five weeks."

"I'm going to be a star," I yelled. I pulled Noreen off the bed, and the two of us skipped around the room in circles, laughing like idiots.

Then Noreen stopped. "You know, it really isn't very nice of us to be celebrating poor Wella Mae's accident. Sister Mary Ignatius says we should never profit from another man's misfortune." We both forced ourselves to look serious for a second.

"Poor Wella Mae," Noreen said.

"Poor *dear* Wella Mae," I added.

Then we both exploded and fell on the bed, laughing.

"What's going on in here?" Mom asked, coming in without knocking. I guess she figured it wasn't my room anymore, so why knock.

"Cat has great news for you, Mrs. Corwin, and I have to get home to watch the boys or Mom will have a fit." Noreen ran out of the room, then stuck her head back in to say, "Congratulations on the extra baby, Mrs. Corwin."

"The extra baby?"

"You know, the third one," Noreen said, then disappeared.

Mom smiled. "Oh. That one. Thank you, Noreen." Mom turned to me. "Didn't Noreen know about the triplets before this, Cat?"

"No. I wanted to save it as a surprise."

"Oh. That's nice." Mom looked as if she might sit down on my bed, then changed her mind. It's a good thing. Last time she did that, I had to call Dad to help me get her up again. "So—what's all this about good news?"

"Wella Mae Riddle broke her arm, and she's in the hospital. I'm going to be the ringmaster."

"What a shame. It must have been a bad fracture to put her in the hospital."

"Yeah, four places," I said. "But you're not getting the message here, Mom. I'm Wella Mae's understudy. I'm getting her part. Isn't that terrific?"

"Well, I'm sure you'll enjoy having the spotlight for a change, Cat, but I don't like to see you gloating over another person's misfortune like this."

All of a sudden I had Sister Mary Ignatius for a mother. "I thought you'd be happy for me."

"Of course I'm happy for you, honey. What about the ringmaster dance? Have you learned it?"

"Sure, I know all the steps, but now that I'm really going to do it, I have to practice it a lot more. Are you sure you have to make my room into the nursery? I won't have any place to practice now."

"I know how much this space means to you, Cat, and if there was any way your Dad and I could fit our bed into the sewing room, I'd make our room into the nursery."

"Well, do you have to change it over right away? Could I have my dance studio at least until the recital? It's only a month away."

Mom sighed. "I don't dare wait any longer. It's getting harder and harder for me to do things. Dr. Braxton says we might have less than a month before the babies arrive." She looked around the room. "There is one possibility, though."

"What's that?"

"Well, the walls in this room were painted fairly recently, so all we really need to do is move your furniture out and the baby furniture in. As long as we know where everything is going to fit, I don't see why we couldn't line the bassinets and dressers up against the wall the way you have your things now. You could leave the mirrors up, and you'd still have the middle of the room to practice in until the babies come home."

"Oh, Mom. That would be great!" I tried to hug her, but it wasn't easy. My hands barely reached around the sides of what used to be her waist. And I could have sworn I felt a little foot kick me.

Chapter Seven

From then on Noreen helped me almost every day with the ringmaster solo. I was getting pretty good, and I was working so hard, it made the rest of May and the first half of June practically fly by. Before we knew it, school was out, and it was a week before the recital—dress rehearsal night.

"Are you sure you have everything, Cat?" Mom asked, as we put my dance stuff in the car.

"Everything's here except the ringmaster costume, Mom, and Madame said she'd have that for me at the rehearsal."

"How do you know it's going to fit? Are you and Wella Mae the same size?"

"Pretty close. She's a little bit taller, but that shouldn't make any difference."

"Probably not, but I'll fix it for you if it isn't right."

"Great, Mom. You sure you don't want to change your mind and come see the dress rehearsal?"

"I don't think I should, Cat. I'm feeling awfully tired today, and the doctor said I should get as much rest as possible. Besides, I'd rather be surprised and just see the performance. I'm really looking forward to next Saturday night." She kissed me good-bye. "When you get home, I'll have some hot chocolate waiting, and you can tell me all about how everything went."

"With lots of marshmallows?" I asked. That was my favorite good-night snack, even in summer.

"With tons of marshmallows."

Mom stood in the driveway, waving as we pulled out. Even with the babies on her mind, Mom had worked hard to get me ready for the recital. It hadn't been easy for her to sew my costumes this year. For the past few weeks she could barely get close enough to the sewing machine to see what she was doing. The *Swan Lake* costume was beautiful, though—a white satin bodice with gathered layers of white net for the skirt. The Rainbow Dance costume was just like it except for the color. It made me look like a head of lettuce, but I didn't tell Mom that. I didn't want to hurt her feelings. It wasn't her fault that the costume had to be green.

Dress rehearsal was terrific. All of a sudden I was a big shot instead of just one of the thundering herd. Even the *Swan Lake* dance went off without a hitch. The Circus Dance was the best part though, and

Wella Mae's costume was almost a perfect fit. I couldn't wait to show Mom.

Alison and Cara came up to me after the rehearsal was over, still wearing their circus pony costumes with the pink plumes in their hair.

"You make a great ringmaster, Cat."

"Thanks, Alison."

"You're twice as good as Wella Mae was," Cara said. "She always looked as if she was bored to death. After all, a circus is supposed to be fun."

Twice as good as Wella Mae! I couldn't wait to tell Mom that one. Parents were arriving, and people were packing up to leave, but there was no sign of Dad. When Noreen and I were the only two kids left, I called home on the pay phone in the hall and let it ring about fifteen times, but there was no answer.

"Do you girls need a ride?" Madame asked. She had her car keys out, and I could tell she was anxious to lock up and go home.

"I don't know what happened, Madame. Dad's always early when he comes to pick me up."

"We could call my mom," Noreen suggested. "She can leave the boys long enough to come get us."

Just then Dad came rushing in. "Sorry I'm late, kids. Something came up. Let's go."

Noreen and I followed him and climbed into the backseat, piling our costumes up on our laps.

"What happened, Dad?"

"It's your mother, Cat. I had to take her to the hospital."

I practically jumped over the seat. "Did she have the babies already?"

"No, but they want her to stay in the hospital until she does. It's too early for them to be born. They aren't ready to live on their own yet, so the doctors are going to keep your mother very quiet and hope the babies don't arrive for a few more weeks."

"A few weeks! You mean she can't come to the recital?"

"Not a chance, Cat," Dad said. I could see his eyes in the rearview mirror. They looked tired and worried. "I know you're disappointed. Your mother is, too. She was looking forward to seeing you dance."

Nobody said anything after that. Even when we dropped Noreen off, she just looked at me and shook her head.

"Can we have some hot chocolate, Dad?" I asked, when we got into the house. "I could tell you about the rehearsal."

Dad rubbed his forehead. "I'm really beat, Cat. Things are just happening too fast lately. Another time, okay?"

"Sure, Dad. Good night."

I'd really been looking forward to my hot-chocolate session with Mom, but it wouldn't have been the same with Dad anyway. I was still too fired up from the rehearsal to go to sleep, so I poked through the kitchen cupboards. I fixed myself a bowl of cereal and went out onto the back steps.

It was a warm night, and the moon was almost full. I started to eat some cereal, but then I got thinking about Mom not being able to go to the recital. She'd always been there for me before, coming to see every recital and every stupid little school performance since kindergarten. Warm tears started sliding down my cheeks. I wasn't crying just because Mom would miss the recital. I was crying because I'd never be as important to either Mom or Dad as I had been while I was growing up. I wasn't their only child anymore. I was just one of four kids.

I heard something move in the bushes, then saw a familiar pair of green eyes glowing in the light from the kitchen window. The cat was back.

I set my cereal bowl down on the ground at my feet and waited. The cat crept across the yard. I could tell he was still hungry, but he had really fattened up. Maybe the daily snacks I'd been leaving by the bushes were paying off. I tried not to move a muscle as he came closer. He watched me at first while he lapped the milk out of the bowl, but then he got too interested in eating and seemed to relax.

I heard a rattling sound as he ate. "Hey, you're purring," I whispered.

The cat moved his ears back and forth a few times,

but he kept on eating. When he finished, he washed his face with his paw, then brushed against my leg and actually let me pet him.

I picked him up and rubbed my cheek against his soft fur. He started licking my face with his scratchy tongue. "I'm going to take you into the house," I said. "You'll be the one thing in the world that just belongs to me."

I carried the cat up to my new room and got ready for bed. The bed and desk took up so much space, my dresser had to be out in the hall. The vanity, with its fancy ruffled skirt had to be stored in the attic until we could figure out what to do with it. Even with just the two pieces of furniture left there was barely space in the middle of my floor to turn around, much less do a pirouette.

It didn't bother the cat, though. He wandered around sniffing everything, then jumped up on my bed and settled into the folded-up quilt at the bottom.

When I turned off my light and climbed into bed, I could see the cat's whiskers glistening in the patch of moonlight coming through my window. "I have to call you something besides 'the cat,'" I whispered. The green eyes looked at me and blinked. "Besides, that's my name. Isn't that silly? A person named Cat? Hey . . . you could be a cat named Person. Only we could spell it P-u-r-r-s-o-n."

The name fit. Purrson stretched his legs out in front of him and kneaded the quilt with his paws, as if he liked the name, too. I forgot about the recital and the babies and closed my eyes, falling asleep to the sound of his purring.

Chapter Eight

"Can you see anybody?" Noreen whispered.

"I'm trying. Hold on." I squinted through the slit in the curtain and searched through the first few rows of the audience. "Your family's here. They're taking up the whole third row." It always surprised me to see Noreen's father. He was almost never at home. He didn't look too happy to be here, either. The McNulty kids were lined up down the row, except for Patrick, who was in his mother's lap.

"Hurry up," Noreen said. "Let me take a peek."

"Wait a second. I can't find my dad." I moved back and forth trying to see the other side of the auditorium through the slit, but I didn't dare touch the curtain. Madame would have had a fit if she knew we were peeking at the audience. She said it was "unprofessional."

"Come on, Cat. It's almost time to start. Madame will be here any minute."

"Wait. Here he comes." I saw Dad hurry down through the auditorium and slip into the only empty seat in the front row, the last one over by the side aisle. Noreen just had time for one quick peek before the other kids came on stage and Madame told us to take our places for the Rainbow Dance.

It's funny how fast things happen once a recital starts. You spend months learning a dance and practicing it over and over, and then you get on stage recital night, and it's over in three or four minutes. My final position in the Rainbow Dance was way over on the left side of the stage. I could see Dad smiling and clapping, and I gave him a big smile back.

Everything went without a hitch after that until it came to the *Swan Lake* number. The curtain opened, and the four of us were standing in center stage with our arms crossed, but the music didn't start. There was some static, then silence. We just stood there like idiots.

"Smile," Alison hissed through clenched teeth.

I was smiling so hard my cheeks ached, when I noticed a man rushing down the aisle on the side where Dad was sitting. He went all the way to the front and bent down to talk to Dad. Then Dad got up. He was leaving!

Just then the music started and the other three girls took off. I tried to catch up, but it was impossible. They zigged, I zagged. They were up, I was down. I could hear giggling in the audience. Then, when we were supposed to do some fast steps on pointe, I lost my balance and pulled down hard on Alison's and Cara's hands. They both fell and took Kim and me with them. We landed in a heap of white net and swan feathers.

The curtain closed before the music ended, and we could hear the audience clapping and laughing.

"I hate you, Cat Corwin," Alison said, trying to untangle herself from my net skirt. "I'll never be in another dance with you as long as I live."

Noreen ran over to me when I got back to the dressing room. "What happened? I heard *Swan Lake* was a disaster."

I was trying to wipe the black streaks of mascara off my face where it had run from my crying. "It's Dad," I said. "He left."

"Well, he must have had a good reason. Besides, how could that make you screw up the dance?"

"Look. You have about forty-five relatives out in that audience. I had one, and now he's gone. So I might as well just forget the whole thing and go home."

"You can't go home. You still have to do the ringmaster."

"Let somebody else do it."

Noreen grabbed my shoulders. "You're the understudy, remember? Nobody else knows the dance."

"You do. And Margo Vinetti is your understudy for the trainer of the circus ponies. She could do your part."

Noreen's thumbs pressed into my shoulders. "Just because your parents aren't here, you're going to give up the dance you would have killed for a month ago? If you do, Madame will never give you a lead again, you know. The *Swan Lake* thing was an accident that could happen to anybody, but Madame would never forgive you for this."

I didn't say anything, and Noreen stared at me for a minute. It seemed funny to see her with dark eyeliner and mascara. Usually her eyelashes were pale red, and you could hardly see them. Then her eyes narrowed, and she took her hands off my shoulders, giving me a little shove as she did. "I guess you're right after all. You do have a way to chicken out if you want to."

"I'm not chickening out. I just don't care about it anymore," I said.

Noreen and I stood there glaring at each other for a minute or two longer. Then she said, "You know darn well you care about this, Cat Corwin. Now stop being a baby and get into your ringmaster costume."

And I did.

I wiped everything out of my mind and just concentrated on doing my best in the circus dance. The part where I do leaps across the whole stage went better than it ever had before. The audience clapped right in the middle of the dance. Then we did our final curtain calls, and the recital was over.

All of the other kids were surrounded by their families in the dressing room, so I just slipped into the girls' bathroom and changed fast, then went back out and packed up my stuff. Pretty soon the McNulty clan came into the dressing room. They all hugged Noreen, then Ryan and Billy came over to me. "Boy, were you ever funny in the duck dance," Ryan said.

Billy bobbed his head up and down. "That was the best thing in the whole recital."

Mrs. McNulty was right behind them and hugged me. "They're right, Cat. I'm glad to see Madame Yvette putting a little humor into these recitals. The rest is pretty and all, but it gets a little boring."

"But it wasn't supposed to be . . ."

Just then Madame Yvette came up to us.

"I know what you're going to say, Madame Yvette," I said. "But the *Swan Lake* thing was . . ."

"Was a great success," Madame said, smiling. "You've added a whole new dimension to our recitals, Catherine, one we'll have to continue, I'm afraid. But right now I have a message for you. Your father called and asked if you could stay with Noreen for the night." She turned to Noreen's mother. "If that's a problem, Mrs. McNulty, I can take Catherine home with me."

"No problem at all," Mrs. McNulty said. "We hardly notice one more in our house."

"But where's Dad?" I asked. "Did something happen to Mom?"

Madame beamed. "He said the babies are being born. You may be a big sister already."

I looked over at Noreen. Michael and Danny were behind her, making faces, Ryan and Billy were under the skirt of her lettuce costume, fighting, and Patrick was by the mirror, drawing a huge clown smile on his face with a stick of blue eyeshadow.

"Yeah," I said. "A big sister at last. That's terrific."

Chapter Nine

"Cat! Noreen! Come down here quick. There's something in the paper you have to see." It took a minute for me to wake up and realize that I was in Noreen's tiny room in the attic of her house, and the voice was Mrs. McNulty's, yelling from the kitchen. It took another minute or two for me to remember why I was here instead of home.

Noreen and I stumbled down the two flights to the kitchen, where all of the McNulty kids were gathered around the kitchen table, even Patrick, sitting in his high chair. Mrs. McNulty was feeding him a dish of oatmeal.

Danny was trying to sound out a word in the newspaper headline. "Kwa . . . kwad . . . rup . . . let . . ."

"*Roop*, not *rup*," Billy said. "It's quad*rup*lets, dummy."

"It says *R-U-P*. That's *rup*," Danny insisted. "Like run."

Noreen grabbed the paper away from her brothers. "Oh my gosh, Cat. Look! It's your mom and dad."

There was a picture of Mom in a hospital bed with Dad sitting next to her, holding her hand. They were both smiling as if it was the happiest day in their lives. Above them, the headline said: Quadruplets Born to Local Couple.

"What's a quadruplets?" Danny asked. "I thought Cat's ma was having a baby."

Noreen looked over at me and rolled her eyes. "She did. Only she had four of them."

Mrs. McNulty shook her head. "Four babies at once. I wish I'd thought of that. You'd all be out of diapers by now."

"Most of us are, Ma," Billy said, grinning.

"Listen to this," Noreen said. "The Corwin family increased from two to six members last evening with the birth of quadruplets. The babies, weighing in at . . ." She stopped and looked at me. "It should have been from three to seven. They're not counting you."

"Let me see that," I said. Noreen and I elbowed the boys out of the way and read the rest of the article to ourselves. "There's nothing about me at all," I whispered to Noreen. It was as if I didn't exist.

Mrs. McNulty hugged me. "Don't fret over a little mistake in the newspaper, Cat. They don't bother to get their facts straight half the time."

"Maybe Cat's ma don't need her no more since she

got all them new babies," Mike said.

Mrs. McNulty gave Mike a halfhearted swat on the rear. "You hush, Michael John McNulty. Cat's ma is going to need her all the more, now that she'll have so many little ones to look after." I felt Noreen's elbow in my ribs.

"I never even heard of a human bean having four babies at once," Billy said. "Only animals can do that."

"Human be-ing," Noreen corrected.

"Besides, four babies is a litter," Billy said, ignoring his sister. "Human beans aren't supposed to have litters."

I glared at him.

"Here's a picture of the babies on the first page of the next section," Mrs. McNulty announced. "Oh, aren't they sweet little things?"

Everybody pushed in at once, and a glass of milk got knocked over. Mrs. McNulty jumped up and grabbed a sponge from the sink. "Noreen! Get the mop and clean up what spilled on the floor," she ordered.

There was a solid wall of McNulty heads between me and the picture. I didn't want to see it anyway. As a matter of fact, a picture of those babies was about the last thing in the world I wanted to see at the moment.

I felt as if I were in a dream world. I stood there

watching Patrick pick up oatmeal from his dish and dribble it carefully in little peaks on the heads of his brothers as they leaned over the table. They all had such thick curly hair they never even felt it.

Patrick smiled at me. I smiled back. The little peaks of oatmeal kept building up, like the towers of a sand castle. It seemed as if Patrick and I were the only two real people in the room. The rest were in a dream—a nightmare with four babies. Pretty soon I'd wake up, and everything would be back the way it was supposed to be. Just me and Mom and Dad. No babies.

"They're all in little glass boxes," Mike said.

Danny wiggled in closer. "Hey, neat! They came gift-wrapped."

"Those are isolettes," Mrs. McNulty explained, running water into the sink. "If babies are real small when they're born, they have to be kept warm. Like these babies. The paper said they only weighed a couple of pounds each. The littlest one didn't even weigh that much."

"What did I weigh when I was born, Ma?" Danny asked. "Did I come in a little box like that?"

Ryan burst out laughing. "You? You were a moose! Right, Ma?"

Mrs. McNulty chuckled. "I'll say he was. Over nine pounds. Now you boys clear out and give Cat a chance to look at that picture. The babies are her brothers, you know." She turned back from the sink just in time to see Patrick putting the finishing touches on the second peak on Danny's head. "Patrick!" she shouted.

Patrick jumped and misfired, letting the gray blob land on the newspaper. Billy turned to Danny. "You should see yourself. You have oatmeal horns on your head."

"So do you, stupid," Danny yelled, giggling. "And Ryan, too."

All four boys began flicking the oatmeal out of their hair and onto each other. Patrick loved it. He giggled and started zinging little oat missiles across the table. Mrs. McNulty scooped him up from the high chair. "You boys get into the backyard and clean yourselves up with the hose. You're acting like a pack of wild animals."

Ryan started howling like a wolf, and the others joined in as they ran outside. Then we could hear water splatting against the side of the house as they wrestled with the hose, laughing and howling.

Mrs. McNulty chuckled as she toweled off Patrick. "Those boys can think of more ways to get into trouble. But what can you expect? Boys will be boys. I'm taking Patrick upstairs to change him, Noreen. See to this mess, will you?"

Noreen rinsed out a sponge, then tossed it over to

me. "Here. You could use some practice in cleaning up. You'll be doing a lot of it from now on."

"It's not going to be the same with my mom, Noreen. We may have four babies, but I'm not going to get stuck with all the work the way you do."

"Ha!" Noreen said. "That's what they all say."

I started to wipe up the table and came to the newspaper. It was soaked with milk, and there were disgusting blobs of oatmeal all over it. I tried to wipe off the picture of the babies, but it was so dark from the wet, it almost looked like the sonogram—except now there were four little goblins instead of three.

Noreen stood across the table from me, her hands on her hips. "So were you lying to me again, Cat?"

"Lying about what?"

"What do you think? Four babies instead of three."

"Believe me, Noreen. I'm as surprised as you are. Mom and Dad didn't even know."

Just then the phone rang. Noreen answered it and handed me the receiver.

"Cat? Did you hear the news?" It was Dad.

"Yeah. I saw it in the paper."

"Four babies, Cat. Do you believe it? For someone who couldn't have children, your mother really did it, didn't she?"

Overdid it was more like it. "Yeah, Dad. Great. Is Mom okay?"

"She's terrific. And you have to see the babies, Cat. They're so tiny, but they're doing fine. I'll come pick you up at the McNulty's."

I needed some time to be alone before I saw those babies. "Let me go home and change first, Dad. I slept in my clothes from yesterday. Come home in about an hour, okay?"

"Sure, honey. The spare key is hanging in the lilac bush."

The spare key had been in the lilac bush for the past ten years, but he always told me that. "I know, Dad. See you."

I thanked Mrs. McNulty and headed for home. Our house seemed different already. From now on all the special little places that had always been mine would have little brothers in them. I'd be just like Noreen. The only place where I'd find any privacy would be the bathroom.

I took a shower and put on clean clothes, then went outside. Purrson's food dish was by the steps, and there was still food in it. "Purrson! Here, kitty-kitty. Here, Purr." I called all around his favorite hiding places, but he didn't come out. I went back inside the house and called some more. There was no sign of him.

I was up in my room looking under my bed when I heard the car come into the driveway. I ran down to meet Dad.

"Do you know where Purrson is, Dad?"

"Which person?"

"No, the cat. The one I've been feeding."

Dad still had one foot in the car. "I don't know, honey. He's probably gone to freeload somewhere else. Let's get going. I can't wait for you to see the babies."

"But Purrson wasn't a freeloader. He was my *pet*."

"Cat, he's only been around here for a short time. It isn't that easy to tame a stray. He just adopted us as his family for a while, and now he's moved on."

I climbed into the car, and we took off. Dad babbled about the babies the whole way to the hospital. It was some sort of a big deal about how much weight they were gaining, so I had to hear about every half-ounce. It was like listening to Mom when she was on a diet, only in reverse.

When we got to the hospital, Dad practically ran into the place, dragging me by the hand. "They're in a special section for premature babies," he told me in the elevator. "It would have been better if they could have been born a couple of weeks from now, but Dr. Braxton says they're going to be fine."

"If the doctors know so much, how come they didn't know there were going to be four babies?" I asked.

"They think the smallest one was probably hiding under the others during the sonogram." Great. One of them was being sneaky already.

The elevator door opened, and I could see a glass wall with people crowding around it. There was even a guy with a TV camera.

A pretty woman wearing a ton of makeup came rushing over and held out her hand to Dad. "You're Mr. Corwin, aren't you?"

Dad nodded but didn't get a chance to say anything before she started in again. "I'm Stephanie Bethancourt for TV Five's Look Alive, live coverage of local news stories as they break, and you, Walter Corwin, are live news. So look alive for TV Five! How does it feel to be the father of quadruplets, Mr. Corwin?"

She was sort of shouting as she talked, which I thought was funny, but I figured she might be hard of hearing or something. Then I realized she was holding a microphone out to Dad. There were bright lights shining in our eyes. Dad was sort of speechless for a second or two, so she pulled the mike away and started talking again.

"And this must be your daughter, Catherine, is that right?"

This time she shoved the mike in my face. "Cat," I said.

Stephanie Bethancourt smiled. "I beg your pardon?"

"She said, 'Cat,'" Dad mumbled. "That's her nickname—Cat."

Stephanie was practically smiling her teeth off, but I could tell she thought my name was stupid, and I was sorry I hadn't let it go at Catherine. "I see. How absolutely . . . intriguing. And what are you naming the babies?"

"Fluffy, Muffy, Buffy, and Puffy," I said, smiling back at her.

Old Stephanie Bethancourt never stopped grinning. "I see. How absolutely . . . unusual."

"Cat's just kidding," Dad said. "We still haven't decided on the names."

"Kidding. I see. How absolutely adorable." She was still smiling, but there was a little edge to her voice now. "Let's go look at the babies, shall we?"

We went over to the glass and looked in. There were four babies in little glassed-in cribs. They all had tubes taped to their noses, and one was wearing a tiny blue ski cap.

"Why is that one wearing a hat?" I whispered to Dad. We were close to the glass, so Stephanie Bethancourt couldn't get her microphone in front of us.

"He's the smallest," Dad said. "They're trying to make sure he stays warm. They had all four of them wearing hats right after they were born, but I guess the others don't need them now."

They were the tiniest babies I'd ever seen, all pink with blond fuzz on their heads—except for the one with the hat. You couldn't tell what color hair he had.

I could hear Stephanie Bethancourt saying something into her microphone. Then I realized the camera was on me again. "What does it feel like to become the big sister of four brothers overnight?"

"I don't know yet," I said. "I guess it'll be okay." After all, they were kind of cute.

"How absolutely philosophical." Stephanie whipped around to face the camera. "That's the story of an absolutely zip-ah-de-do-dah event for the Corwin family. We'll be giving you periodic updates on the Corwin quads. For now, I'm Stephanie Bethancourt for TV Five's Look Alive."

The lights went off, and other reporters started crowding around us. Dad said they'd have to wait because he was taking me to see my mother.

Mom was asleep when we went into her room, but she opened her eyes when I sat down by the bed.

"Hi, honey. Did you see the babies?"

"Yeah. They're really cute. How are you feeling?"

Mom grinned. "Wonderful. I can see my feet again. Your father and I were starting to think of names, Cat, but we wanted you to help. We have to come up with something. The nurses are calling them A,B,C, and D."

"That's catchy," I said.

"Now be serious and help, Cat. I want the names to be individual, no cutesy gimmicks like starting with the same letter."

"She had some great suggestions on TV just now," Dad said. "How about Fluffy, Buffy, Muffy, and Puffy?"

"Cat, you didn't," Mom said, laughing.

"Well, that lady made me mad," I said. "You know the one. From Channel Five."

"Ah yes, Stephanie Bethancourt. She interviewed me within an hour of the babies' birth. I have no idea what I said to the woman. Anyway, getting back to names. What do you think of these?"

She held out a list. We talked about boys names for the next hour, and finally decided on Seth, Ian, Tim, and Max.

In all that time, Mom and Dad never once asked about my dance recital.

Chapter Ten

Mom had to stay in the hospital for the rest of the week. Dad and I visited her every night. When we went in to see the babies, we had to wash our hands with a special soap and put on masks and gowns. It was hard to find a gown for me that didn't drag on the floor, but the nurses showed me how to double it over at the waist when I tied it, so I wouldn't trip on it.

Pretty soon I could tell the babies apart, not by how they looked but by the way they acted. Seth was the biggest, and he was usually sleeping. Then there was Ian, who was always moving an arm or a leg, even when he was asleep. Tim cried the most and stopped only when he was sucking on his fist. The one I liked the best was Max. He was the smallest, and they still had him wearing the little blue hat.

Mom finally came home on Friday, but the babies had to stay. Mom said they had to get up to a certain weight before they could leave the hospital. The doctor had said it might take five or six weeks.

I'd been looking forward to having Mom come home because it seemed like it had been forever since we'd all been together. But even though it was just the three of us again, things had changed. When I tried to talk to Mom, she seemed so far away, as if she were still back in the hospital with the babies. I knew she was worried about Max, because every morning the first thing she did was call the hospital to see how he had been during the night.

Mom tried to act interested in what I was doing, but she didn't seem to understand how I felt about things—like when she saw me dumping the old food out of Purrson's dish and putting fresh food out for him.

"What are you doing, Cat? You'll have every stray animal in town coming to our door if you keep that up."

"I know Purrson will come back if I keep putting out the food, Mom. It's only been a little over a week."

"You might as well face up to the fact he's gone for good. If you want another cat, we'll go to the animal shelter and get one."

"I don't want just any cat, Mom. I want Purrson."

"Well, I think you're being stubborn and foolish. That cat is probably miles from here by now." She went back into the house, letting the screen door slam behind her.

Why couldn't she understand that a new cat wouldn't replace Purrson? If she felt that way, did she think the new babies could take my place? No wonder she didn't seem to care about me the way she used to.

I had to find Purrson now. I picked up the dish and started an all-out search of the yard. Lately I'd just been putting the food out and calling from the back steps. This time I crawled under the bushes around the edge of the yard and called to him. When I got to the far corner of the garden, I thought I heard a faint mewing sound coming from Dad's toolshed. I unhooked the door and pushed it open.

It was dark in the shed except for a single shaft of sunlight coming through the door. I called again, and this time a loud mew answered me. Purrson climbed out from inside a coiled-up hose, stretched, and came over to me.

I scooped him up, rubbing my cheek against the soft fur. "I knew you wouldn't run away. You must have been shut in the toolshed all week." There was a sprinkling can half-full of water by the shed door. "Is this water all you've had to keep you alive, Purrson, or did you catch some mice?" I headed for the house, holding him tight. "You must be starved. I'm going to give you the best meal you've ever had. Then we'll go up to my room and we'll . . . ouch!"

As I reached for the handle of the screen door, Purrson jumped out of my arms, jabbing my shoulder with his claws as he leaped. He headed back toward the toolshed, and I ran after him. "It's okay, Purr," I called. "Don't be afraid, boy." When I looked through the door, he was stepping carefully into the coiled-up hose again, making a deep rumbling sound in his throat and licking something that was down inside the hose. When I looked closer, I saw what it was. Kittens—three of them! There was a gray-and-white one, a yellow tiger, and a little one that looked just like Purrson, all with their eyes still closed.

"Purrson, you're a father!"

Purrson stepped gingerly over the kittens, then settled down inside the hose. The yellow kitten groped around for a few seconds, then pushed up against Purrson's stomach and started to nurse.

"Oh my gosh, Purrson. You're a mother!" At least the name Purrson worked for a boy or a girl.

I picked up the gray-and-white kitten and took it out into the light where I could see it better, then sat down on the back steps, cradling it in my hands. The kitten kept mewing, moving its wobbly little head around. In a flash, Purrson was next to me on the step. He—or rather she—put her front paws on my lap, and I thought she was going to climb up, but she reached over and grabbed the nape of the kitten's neck in her mouth. Then she jumped down and walked across the yard, the kitten swinging back and forth with each step.

"Come back, Purrson," I called. "I'm not going to hurt your babies." She set the baby on the grass for a second and turned to look at me. Then she picked it up and went back into the shed. Her babies were the only thing that mattered to her now.

All kinds of presents had been coming in for the quadruplets, lots of them from people we didn't even know. My old room was completely transformed into a mass-production nursery. My mirrors had been taken down and stored in the basement, and there was no space for dancing in the middle of the floor anymore.

After dinner one night, when Mom had been home for about three weeks, I heard a ticking sound coming from my old room, so I went in. The sound was coming from a couple of those wind-up baby swings. Mom had them both going full blast, with Belinda Suzanne, my Cabbage Patch doll, in one and a stuffed rabbit in the other. Mom was sitting in the rocking chair, feeding a bottle to my baby doll, and Dad was at the changing table putting a Pampers on my teddy bear.

I stood in the doorway. "Have you two gone off the deep end or something?"

Dad popped the teddy bear into a third swing and cranked it up. "This is just a practice drill. We've got this quadruplet thing down to a science."

"If you want to try your hand at this, Ian's ready for his bottle," Mom said, grinning.

"Sure," I said, trying to get into the spirit of things. "Which one's Ian?"

"The bunny."

"I'd feel dumb feeding a bunny. How about Belinda Suzanne?"

Dad handed me a bottle. "That's Seth. He's already been fed."

I picked up the stuffed bunny and sat down in the other rocking chair. "Hi, Ian," I cooed. "What big ears you have."

"The better to hear you with," Mom squeaked in a high baby voice, and we all laughed. It seemed good to be having fun with Mom and Dad again.

As soon as everybody was burped and settled in a crib, we went to the hospital to see the real babies. Max was the one I liked to watch when we went to visit, and I even whispered to him when nobody was listening, telling him what it would be like when he got to come home. There weren't many chances to be alone with him, though, because the nurses were always doing more to him than the others. Mom said there was a problem with his lungs, which made it hard for him to breathe. He stayed very still, and his chest seemed to cave in every time he took a breath. Mom usually spent most of her time with Max, but right now she was busy feeding Seth, and Dad was with Ian. The nurse finished whatever she was doing with Tim and went into the next room, so I pulled a chair up next to Max's isolette.

"Hi. I'm Cat, your big sister, remember?" I whispered. "I'm going to tell you a secret. I have kittens at home. I had this boy cat, and he turned out to be a girl cat, because he had kittens. Actually, that's backwards—he had kittens because he was a girl. Anyway, there are only three kittens, but one of them can be yours. You can choose whichever one you want. I don't think Mom is going to let me keep them all. I've been sneaking food out to them in the toolshed, and I haven't even told her about them yet. Mom has enough to worry about with all you guys showing up. Anyway, when Dad finally gets around to watering the lawn, the jig is up."

Max blinked and kept working hard to breathe.

"Don't get me wrong. Mom is all excited about bringing you home. It's just that first we thought there was just one of you, then two, and then you had to hide when they did the sonogram, so they thought only the other three were in there. You came as a real shock, you know?"

A nurse went by, so I shut up until she got too far away to hear.

"Mom and Dad have it all worked out how they're going to take care of you guys. They've been practicing and everything, so don't worry. Just promise me you're not going to be like Patrick, okay? He's my girlfriend Noreen's little brother, and he's a major brat. One Patrick in a family is too many, but four would be murder."

Max didn't smile or anything, but I had the feeling he knew what I was saying.

Two weeks later Mom got a phone call from the hospital, first thing in the morning. "This afternoon? That's wonderful. Of course we're ready. We've been ready for six weeks. But what about Max?" Her shoulders sagged. "I was afraid of that. All right. I'll call Walter, and we'll be in at about two."

"What's wrong with Max?" I asked.

"Nothing. It's just that he hasn't gained weight as fast as the others, and he still has the breathing problem. Dr. Braxton wants to keep him a while longer. The other three are coming home this afternoon. Your father has made arrangements to take his vacation now, so he'll be home to help."

"That's not fair. Max is going to be lonesome, all by himself," I said, but Mom didn't hear me. She was already dialing Dad's number at work to tell him the news.

Chapter Eleven

Three nurses, each carrying a baby wrapped in a blue blanket, came with us as we headed out of the hospital. I guess hospitals don't want to take a chance on having people drop their babies on hospital property. Anyway, I was glad not to have to carry one because there were reporters and photographers crowding around and flashbulbs going off. Other people were stopping to see what all the fuss was about, so the crowd was growing. If anyone was likely to drop a baby in the confusion, it would be me.

"At least there aren't any TV cameras here," Mom whispered as we turned a corner and headed for the main entrance. "I thought for sure we'd have to contend with Stephanie Bethancourt."

All of a sudden I remembered something. "Oops! I forgot to mention that, didn't I?"

"Mention what?" Mom asked.

"When you went to the store this morning, Stephanie Bethancourt called and asked if she could meet us at the house when we brought the babies home."

"Cat! You didn't say yes, did you?"

"No."

"Well, thank heaven for that. So there's no problem."

"Well, I think there might be a little problem, because I told her she'd have to talk to you or Dad."

Dad put his hand on my shoulder to guide me through the crowd of people as we got to the door. "That was good thinking, Cat."

"But she gave me a phone number, and you were supposed to call her back."

"Well, we didn't," Mom said, "so she won't be there."

I was going to tell them the rest of it, but a newspaper photographer stopped us. "Could you hold it right there, Mr. and Mrs. Corwin? We'd like a picture of you with the babies." He lined up the three nurses with Mom on one end and Dad on the other.

I started to go over next to Mom, but another photographer got in my way. "Watch out, kid. You're going to mess up the shot."

"I'm their sister," I said.

"Whose sister?"

"The quadruplets. They're my baby brothers."

"Yeah, sure, brown eyes. You really look like you belong in a whole family of blue-eyed blonds. Now beat it, will you? Where are your folks anyways?"

Just then Mom called me.

"They're right over there," I said. I slipped in beside Mom and gave the photographer a dirty look. He scratched his head, then started taking pictures along with the other photographers.

Mom and Dad were so busy smiling for the cameras and answering questions, they didn't even notice what had happened. Then they were fussing over getting the babies in the car and fastening them into infant seats that took up almost the whole backseat. I had to squeeze between Seth and Tim. Ian was in my usual spot in the middle of the front seat.

The photographers snapped pictures of the car as we drove away. "I just can't wait to get home to peace and quiet," Mom said, glancing over her shoulder to check on Seth and Tim. "Look at that. The sound of the car's engine seems to be putting them all to sleep."

Everything was nice and quiet until we turned the corner onto our street.

"What's the Channel Five van doing in front of our house? Cat, do you know anything about this?" Mom yelled. That woke Ian up, and he started crying.

"I didn't get a chance to tell you the part where Stephanie Bethancourt said if she didn't hear from us, she'd assume it was all right to come."

Mom moaned. As we pulled into the driveway, the van doors opened. Stephanie Bethancourt and a cameraman were heading toward us. Some of the neighbors were out in their front yards, waiting to see why Channel Five was in the neighborhood.

Dad started to get out of the car, but Stephanie stopped him. "If you wouldn't mind going back to the corner, Mr. Corwin, we'd like to get a shot of you pulling up to the house. Then as you start taking the babies out, we'll follow you inside."

Seth was starting to whimper, and Tim was screwing up his face. Mom leaned over Dad. "If it's all the same to you, Miss Bethancourt..."

Stephanie Bethancourt gave Mom a big flashy smile. "*Ms*. Bethancourt, or better yet, just call me Stephanie. I'm sure we'll be getting to know each other *very* well in the coming months."

Mom leaned over farther, so she wouldn't have to talk so loud. The only problem was, she was still bigger than usual on top, and she leaned on the horn by mistake. All three babies jumped and started howling. "Look, Stephanie. We have three very unhappy babies here, and I'd like to get them into the house as quickly as possible."

Stephanie looked into the backseat. "Three? But there were supposed to be four. Your daughter said you were bringing them all home today. If I'd known there were only going to be three, I wouldn't have brought a whole camera crew out here."

"I didn't say that, Mom. Nobody said how many babies. She was talking about four babies, and I was talking about three babies."

Mom was struggling to get Ian's seat belt untangled from his car seat. "We don't expect Cat to be our press secretary, Stephanie. You should have checked with the hospital. And I'm sorry if three babies aren't enough of a news story for you, but three babies seem to be about all we can handle at the moment." She finally got Ian's car seat loose and handed him to Dad, who had come around to her side of the car.

Stephanie Bethancourt signaled to the cameraman and went into action. "This is Stephanie Bethancourt, from TV Five's Look Alive, coming to you this afternoon from the home of the Corwin quadruplets. This is an absolutely fan*tab*ulous moment for the Corwin family. As you can see, three of the babies are coming home."

Mom opened the back door and was working on Seth's seat belt when I realized that the cameraman was behind her.

"Don't look now, Mom," I yelled over the babies' racket, "but your rear end is on live TV."

"This is all your fault, Cat Corwin," Mom shouted back, yanking at the seat belt. "You're old enough to know how to take and deliver a telephone message." The car seat pulled free, and she handed it, with Seth in it, to Dad. "Where's Ian?"

"I left him on the front steps."

"You *left* him on the steps? On live television? You can't plunk a baby on the steps like a bag of groceries, Walter. They'll be accusing us of child neglect before we ever get them into the house."

"He's six weeks old and strapped into a car seat, Diane. Where the heck do you think he's going to go?"

Stephanie Bethancourt was practically shouting into her microphone. The babies were howling so loudly that any neighbors who had missed seeing the Channel Five van in the first place were coming out on their porches now. "Oh sure," Mom muttered to herself as she hauled Tim out of the other side of the car. "Just all come out and watch the show, why don't you? Don't anybody bother to lend us a hand."

We got all of the babies up to the front steps and were watching Dad go through all his pockets. The whole world was watching Dad go through his pockets. "Darn. I seem to have misplaced my house key. It's on the same key ring as the car keys, Cat. Go back and see if I left them in the ignition."

I ran back down the sidewalk and searched the car, but there was no sign of the keys. The TV camera was on me as I headed back for the house, so I threw in a little twirl and a leap as I got to the front steps. Wella Mae Riddle, eat your heart out! "No keys, Dad."

Dad searched his pockets again. "Do you have your set of keys, Diane?"

"No, I don't have my set of keys. I didn't need them because I wasn't the one who drove, re-member? You said my driving has been too erratic since the babies came, remember? You said . . ."

"You want me to get the spare house key, Dad?" I asked.

Dad looked puzzled. "Spare house key?"

"You know. In the lilac bush out back."

"Oh yes. The spare house key. I forgot."

Forgot? How could he forget? I was beginning to get worried. How were Mom and Dad going to take care of three babies if they couldn't even take care of themselves?

I grabbed the key and took it back to Dad. A small crowd was gathering on our front sidewalk. Mom and Dad took the babies inside, then Mom stuck her head out the door. "Go home, everybody. The show's over."

Stephanie Bethancourt was coming up the side-walk, but Mom slammed the door before she got to it. I ran over and turned on Channel Five. There was Stephanie Bethancourt standing on our front steps, saying something about the absolutely momentous occasion on Mackinberry Street. It was hard to hear her over all the screaming in the house. I ran to the window and waved.

I could see myself on TV for a second. Then they switched to a close-up of Stephanie, and she signed off. The picture flashed back to a soap opera. Channel Five had interrupted "The Guiding Light" for us. I couldn't believe it.

Mom came into the room carrying three bottles. "Each of you pick up a baby and get settled in a comfortable chair." Seth was already calming down, so I chose him. I carried him carefully over to the couch, making sure to support his head the way Mom had shown me. His face was still bright red from crying, and his breath came in little hiccups, but I could tell the worst was over.

Dad wasn't having very good luck with Tim. He was still yelling and his little fists vibrated each time he tanked up with more air. Mom gave each of us a bottle and picked up Ian. It took about a half hour before all three babies were busy drinking and the room was quiet except for the sucking noises.

Mom rested her head on the back of the chair and smiled. "Ah. Blessed peace. If we can just keep our wits about us, I think we'll survive this."

"Don't you think we should reconsider getting

some help with the babies, Diane?" Dad asked.

"No, Walter. You know we can't afford to hire anyone to help."

"But you have a list of people who said they'd volunteer their time."

"That would just make things more complicated,
and you saw how the babies reacted to having all
those extra people around. Everything would have
been fine if the TV people hadn't been here to add to
the confusion." She shot a look at me. "Besides, I
don't want a lot of strangers parading through the
house. If we're really organized, I'm sure we'll be just
fine."

I wanted to say that everything would have been a
lot better if Mom hadn't yelled and leaned on the
horn, but I thought I'd better keep my mouth shut.
Gradually, the babies drifted off to sleep and Mom
took them, one by one, up to the nursery.

Everything was great for about an hour and a half.
Then, right in the middle of dinner, we heard somebody
crying. Then there were two babies crying, and by the
time we got to the top of the stairs, it was a trio.

"Everybody take a baby," Mom ordered.

I grabbed Seth again, but this time it was a bad
choice. He was soaking wet.

"This will be a good chance for you to practice
changing a diaper," Mom said, jiggling Ian up and

down on her shoulder. Dad had put Tim in the swing, and he was howling even louder. "These things work better on teddy bears," Dad said, picking the baby up again.

I put Seth down on the changing table and took off his little suit and diaper. Then, just as I was reaching over him to get a Pampers, I felt something warm hit my neck and trickle down my front. I couldn't believe what had just happened. "Mom!" I yelled. "He peed on me."

"Boy babies do that, Cat. You just have to watch out and keep them covered."

"That's really gross. Patrick throws food, but he's never done anything like this." Since Mom and Dad were busy with their own problems at the moment, I could see I wasn't going to get any sympathy. I mopped up my neck and shirt and kept going. I finally managed to get the diaper on, but it wasn't easy because Seth kept kicking, and the diaper was huge on him. Then I grabbed one of the little stretch suits, only it didn't look so little when I tried to put it on him. The legs of the suit were about six inches longer than Seth's legs. Besides, I'd just get one leg shoved into the pants and he'd kick it out before I could get the other one in. I finally settled on putting both of Seth's legs in one of the pants legs. That slowed down his kicking, but the screaming got worse.

Dad took his turn at the changing table with Tim, and Mom went ahead and changed Ian in his crib. Everybody was still yelling, including Mom and Dad.

"Okay. We tried the diapers," Dad said. "Now what? They certainly couldn't be hungry again. It's not even two hours since their last meal."

"They're not wearing watches, Walter," Mom said. "Get the bottles!"

I sat in the rocking chair and tried giving Seth his bottle, but he kept turning his head back and forth and wouldn't take the nipple. He just screamed.

Dad was jiggling Tim up and down against his chest. "Aren't you supposed to put a wind-up clock in the crib with babies so they think it's the sound of the mother's heartbeat?" he asked.

"For heaven's sakes, Walter. That's for puppies."

I couldn't believe Mom and Dad were so bad at taking care of babies. After all, they'd had me to practice on. Even though it was a while back, they should remember something. "What did you two do with me when I cried?"

"You never did," Dad said.

"Never?"

"Well, not like this, at least. Right, Diane?"

"Definitely not like this. This I would remember."

"I'm going to take Tim into another room," Dad said. "No baby in his right mind would calm down in here."

"That's a good idea," I said. "Mom, can I take Seth out in the backyard?"

"I guess it's warm enough, Cat. We certainly aren't making any progress with all three of them together."

I went out and started walking around the yard holding Seth over my shoulder and rubbing his back. I even tried humming softly to him, but he kept crying, so I had to sing louder, and that just made things worse. I finally gave up and went over to sit on the back steps. "Purrson," I called. "Here, kitty, kitty."

Purrson's head appeared in the doorway of the toolshed, and she approached me cautiously. I think she wondered what sort of squawling animal I had in my lap. I sat Seth up against my stomach so he could see the cat. Purrson came closer and sniffed at Seth's feet. The baby stopped crying, and his eyes got big as he watched her.

"How do you do it, Purrson? You have three babies, and you take care of them all by yourself. We can't even do it with three people, and we still have one more baby to come home. This place is a disaster area."

Purrson rubbed against my leg for a few minutes, but when Seth made a sudden gurgling noise, she jumped and ran back to her own babies. Seth started to cry again. "Some help you are," I yelled after the cat. "Just wait till you're having a bad day with the kittens. See if I give you a hand."

When I went back into the house, Mom and Dad had calmed down the other two. Mom took Seth from me and carried him upstairs. Dad and I turned on the TV in the living room but kept the sound real low so that the babies wouldn't hear it. It was so low *I* couldn't even hear it. We were watching "The Cosby Show" in pantomime.

Mom came down and slumped into the chair. "I'm glad that's over. All our wonderful practice drills were great for dolls and stuffed animals, but live crying babies are a whole different story. I don't know about you two, but I'm going to call it a night and get some sleep while I can."

Mom and Dad went upstairs, but I stayed up to see the end of the show. Then I had a dish of ice cream, brushed my teeth, and climbed into bed. I thought about poor Max, all by himself in the hospital. In all of the times we visited, I never once saw him cry. Boy, were we dumb. We brought home the three screamers and left the quiet baby in the hospital.

I read for a while until I got sleepy. Then, just as I reached over to turn off my light, I heard one of the babies start to cry again.

Chapter Twelve

The next two days were a nightmare. There was never a period of more than a couple of hours, day or night, when one of the babies wasn't crying. If one started, and you didn't get him out of the room in time, he would get the other two going. The swings could keep them happy for about ten minutes, and a bottle was usually good for fifteen. In between, we did a lot of jiggling and diddling and rocking and walking and, most of all, driving.

The one thing that you could count on to put all three babies to sleep at the same time was the car. That first night, we all went out at two in the morning and drove around for about an hour. The babies fell asleep right away, but each time Dad tried to sneak back into the driveway, one of them would wake up, and we'd have to start out again. That night Mom, Dad, and the babies made a second trip out at five, but I stayed home and got the only solid hour of sleep I had that night.

By the third day everybody's nerves were frazzled. In the morning Mom and Dad took the babies to the pediatrician to see if there was any reason why they cried so much. He said there was nothing wrong with them, and we just needed to get them on a reasonable schedule. Easy for him to say. The babies were the ones who weren't being reasonable.

As if things weren't bad enough, Mom went poking into the toolshed for something, then came storming back into the house.

"Cat! Did you know that stray cat you've been feeding has had a litter of kittens in our toolshed?"

"Yeah, Mom. I was waiting for a good time to tell you, but there haven't been a whole lot of good times lately."

"You certainly didn't think you were going to keep them, I hope."

"Aw, Mom, please? I've never had a pet before, and I promise I'll take care of them."

"That isn't the point. We can't have five children and four cats in one house. As soon as the kittens are old enough to leave their mother, you'll have to find homes for them."

"How about we just keep Purrson and two of the kittens?"

"No."

"One kitten?"

"No!"

Mom didn't follow that up with "absolutely not," so I figured there was still some hope.

The babies got real fussy that afternoon, so we packed them off for a ride until they slept. Then Mom and Dad settled them all down in their cribs. While they were upstairs, I heard the clank of the mailbox lid, so I went out to see what had arrived. In the middle of a pile of bills there was an envelope from Madame Yvette's studio. I had forgotten that the summer session would be starting soon. At least that was something to look forward to—two weeks of daily dance classes. What a great way to end the summer.

I'd have to call Noreen the first chance I got. Things had been so hectic, I'd only talked to her once on the phone, and I'd had to cut that short when Mom called me to help with the screamers.

Mom and Dad were at the kitchen table having a cup of coffee when I came back in. "We've put more miles on the car this week than we did when we took the trip to the Grand Canyon," Dad said. "Nobody told me that the biggest expense with these babies would be gas."

"We should trade in the house for one of those

motor homes," I said, handing him the mail. "Then every time somebody cried, you could just drive around the block. We wouldn't even have to interrupt dinner."

"Not a bad idea," Dad said, opening the first few bills. His face looked more and more worried as he went through the pile.

"There's one in there from Madame Yvette," I said. "Summer session starts next week."

Dad set it aside without even opening it. "I'm afraid you're going to have to pass up the dance lessons this summer, Cat. I can barely manage the bills for the essentials. We'll have to do without the extras until we get back on our feet."

"But dancing *is* essential, Dad. I'll eat a lot less or wear old clothes or something to save the money, but don't make me give up the dancing now. I'm just starting to get good."

"There's nothing more to discuss, Cat. I can't pay for dance lessons right now, and that's final." He got up and went out the back door.

"Mom! You've got to say something to change his mind."

Mom's face looked grim. "Your father's right, Cat. We all knew we'd have to make sacrifices for these babies, and the bills already have been astronomical. You're old enough to understand the situation. Maybe you can start up with the lessons later in the year."

"You don't have any idea how important this is to me, do you? Do you realize that in all the time you've been home since the babies were born, you've never once asked me how my recital went?"

"I'm sorry, Cat. Things have just been so over-whelming lately. . . ."

"Why am I making all the sacrifices? You didn't even have to give up your room. My whole life has changed, and I'm getting stuck with as much of the work as you and Dad are."

"If we'd just had one baby, everything would have been simple, Cat. Having quadruplets has compli-cated our lives, but we'll work it out if you can just be patient. We knew the medication I was on might re-sult in more than one baby, but we never dreamed that . . ."

"Wait a minute. What do you mean? Have other people who had these shots had quadruplets?"

"Well, multiple births are a possible side effect. Some of the women have even had quintuplets."

"You knew that, and you went ahead and took them anyway? Why? Did you want another baby that much? Wasn't I good enough for you?"

"Stop this nonsense, Cat. You know how much we love you. It's just that we wanted to have a child of . . ."

She stopped, but I knew what she was going to say. "Of your own?"

"That's not what I meant. You're as much our own child as if I'd given birth to you. You know that."

"I *don't* know that. I hear all these people fussing over the babies and saying this one has Dad's nose, and that one has your eyes. That's what you wanted, wasn't it? To see what your own kid would look like? Nobody knows *who* my nose came from. Nobody even cares."

"Cat, that's not true." Mom got up and tried to put her arms around me, but I pushed her away.

"What you did wasn't fair. You knew about those shots, and you went ahead anyway and had a whole stupid litter. Even the cat only had three kittens. She has more sense than you do."

That's when she slapped me, but I couldn't stop.

"I hate you," I screamed. "I hate you for ever adopting me in the first place. Why didn't you just leave me alone?"

"That's what comes from being an only child all these years," Mom shouted. "You're spoiled rotten. It's about time you had some brothers. Maybe now you'll start thinking about somebody besides yourself for a change."

Her words struck me like a pail of ice water. I ran blindly out the back door, letting it slam behind me. I could hear the babies starting up again, but I didn't care. They weren't my babies, and I wasn't going to get stuck taking care of them. This wasn't my family anymore.

Chapter Thirteen

Noreen was out in the backyard, hanging up a load of wash when I got there. I was so out of breath from running, I could barely talk.

"Cat! What's the matter? You look awful."

"You were right all along, Noreen," I gasped. "The babies have wrecked my life. I'm never going back there."

"Really?" Noreen's eyes got wide, but she had just a hint of an I-told-you-so smile on her face. "Come in the house and tell me what happened."

"No. I don't want anybody to hear about this."

"Don't worry. Nobody's home. Mom went shopping with my aunt Kate, and they took Patrick along. The rest of the boys went to the carnival. Ryan's new best friend is this rich kid, Ronnie Jablonski. His father said he'd take Ryan and my other brothers."

"Why didn't you go?"

Noreen made a face. "With Ronnie Jablonski? I'd rather eat toads. Come on."

We went into the kitchen and Noreen poured us each a glass of green Kool-Aid. "Did you really mean it about not going back home?"

"There's no way I'll go back. The babies scream all day and all night. And now Dad says I have to give up dance lessons, at least for now."

"You're kidding!"

"No, I'm not. And that's not all." I gave her a blow-by-blow of the past three days. She just sat there staring at me, blowing bubbles and popping them as she shook her head in amazement.

"If you're not going back home, where are you going to live?"

"Here," I said.

Noreen popped a huge bubble. "Here? Are you crazy? Do I look like I'm living the life of a princess here?"

"Well, where else can I go? All of Mom's and Dad's relatives live on the West Coast. I can't exactly hop on a plane and show up on their doorstep. Besides, they're not even related to me."

"What about finding your real mother?" Noreen asked. "There was a story on TV the other night where a girl did that, and it turned out great."

"If my real mother didn't want me when I was little

and cute, why would she want me now?"

Noreen studied my face as she picked pieces of bubble gum off her nose and cheeks. "Yeah. I see what you mean. Besides, I need to get away, too. We have to find a place where we can go together."

"Why do we have to go anyplace? If I lived here with you, I could help you with the work. Doing everything together would be fun, and we'd finish up twice as fast as when you do everything by yourself. Besides, even if your brothers are creeps, at least they don't cry all the time or pee on you."

"That's about all they don't do," Noreen said, starting to flip through the newspaper. "I know you can't live here, though."

"Why not?"

"Where do you think you'd sleep? My room is about the size of a postage stamp."

I'd forgotten about that. Noreen was probably the only kid in the world who had a room smaller than mine. It was a tiny finished-off corner in the attic. "Well, I could always sleep on your couch."

Noreen kept looking through the newspaper. "No way. Pa sleeps on the couch every time he and Ma have a fight, and that's about twice a week."

"What do you think you're going to find in that newspaper? An ad offering a home for two kids who want to run away?"

"Here it is." Noreen folded the paper back and

smoothed it out in front of her.

"Here *what* is?"

"We'll find the answer in our horoscopes. The big movie stars make all their important decisions that way."

"Great. We all know how gloriously happy they are," I said, picturing the newspapers at the A&P checkout counter.

"Here's mine: 'Taurus—A career change is in the offing. Take advantage of an opportunity that will put you in the public eye.'"

"Yeah, like a sty," I mumbled.

She ignored me. "Here's yours: 'Scorpio—Your artistic tendencies can take you far. Embark upon a decorative project.'"

"Come on, Noreen. Everybody will be home pretty soon. If we're going anywhere, we'd better get out now."

"We can't leave until we understand the message. We don't know where we're supposed to go."

"That stuff doesn't mean anything," I said. "In the first place, you don't even have a career to change."

"Sure I do. I'm a professional slave. Hey, look what's right next to the horoscopes on this page. It must be an omen."

I looked over her shoulder. "It's just a story about the Constantine Family Carnival. Big deal. That's where your brothers went, isn't it?"

"Don't be so dense, Cat. A carnival is in the public eye, right?" She didn't wait for me to answer. "Now for the artistic talent part."

"Carnival posters?" I suggested.

Noreen leaned back and squinted her eyes. She pulled a long string of gum out of her mouth, then wound it up on her index finger and shoved it back in. She always did that when she was deep in thought. "No, it has to be something decorative that would help us join the carnival. Something that would take us far... something decorative like... like tattoos! We'll be tattooed ladies. It's perfect."

"I don't want to slow you down when you're on a roll, Noreen, but I don't have a single tattoo and neither do you."

"We'll draw our own. I have a great set of markers. They'll never be able to tell the difference."

"Yeah, until the first rain."

"That doesn't matter. We just need to be convincing enough to get the jobs. We aren't really going to join the carnival."

"We aren't?"

Noreen rolled her eyes. "Of course not, silly. We only need to run away for a few days—just long enough for our parents to miss us and appreciate us."

"But how's that going to change anything? The work will still be there when we get back."

"Sure it will, but we won't get stuck doing all of it, because our running away will teach them a lesson."

"Yeah, I see what you mean. They'll feel guilty about the way they treated us, right?"

Noreen jumped up from the table. "Give that lady a cigar!" she shouted.

"But you're forgetting a couple of things, Noreen. First of all, nobody hires eleven-year-old kids for anything but baby-sitting and mowing the lawn. And even if they did, the carnival isn't going to give us jobs for just a couple of days."

"I've already thought of that. We can fix ourselves up to look like we're eighteen. Ma has all kinds of clothes, high-heeled shoes, and jewelry packed away right outside my room in the attic. And we're not going to let the carnival know we only want the job for a few days. When they get ready to leave town, we'll just tell them we forgot that we get really carsick, and we're very sorry but we have to quit."

"Okay, that sounds good, but what if the carnival already has a tattooed lady?"

"Then we need a gimmick." Noreen pulled her gum out to a long thread, then sucked it in like a piece of spaghetti. "We'll be tattooed dancing ladies. We'll call ourselves the . . . Decorative Dancing Dolly Sisters."

That one made me laugh out loud. "Sisters?"

Noreen glared at me. "Well, cousins then."

"This is never going to work, Noreen. Nobody's going to give us a job. And besides, running away to join the carnival is so corny. It's like the plot of a bad movie."

"Do you have any better ideas? This article makes the people sound really nice. A lot of them are related to the owner, Stavros Constantine. It says here that they're one of the few small traveling carnivals left. This is probably our last chance to get away."

"I don't know."

Noreen stared at me, then popped a bubble. "You have a choice, Cat. It's either the carnival or those screaming babies."

When she put it that way, the decision was easy. "Okay," I said. "You win."

"Great! We probably have about an hour and a half before everybody gets back," Noreen said. "Ma and Aunt Kate always get talking and forget the time. Let's pick out our clothes first." We went up to the attic, dragged a big carton into Noreen's room and started going through it.

"Isn't your mother going to be mad at us for taking her stuff?" I asked.

"She'll never miss any of it. She hasn't looked in those cartons for years. Ma couldn't fit into these now, anyway. She's just saving them in case she loses weight."

I held a bright yellow sleeveless dress up in front of

me. It came only halfway to my knees. "Did your mother really wear this stuff?"

"Sure." Noreen had put on a pink dress with purple bands around the bottom and the armholes. Hers was even shorter than mine.

"Is your mother an ex-midget or something?"

"This stuff is from the sixties—miniskirts. Ma says if you keep stuff around long enough, it comes back into style. Like it's doing now."

I tried to picture Mrs. McNulty in a miniskirt, but I couldn't quite manage it. I pulled off my T-shirt and shorts and slipped into the yellow dress. Noreen squinted at me, then dove back into the box and started slinging things over her shoulder. "Here," she said, surfacing again. "You'll need this." She tossed something black and lacy to me.

I caught it. It was a bra. "What are you, crazy? The last thing either one of us needs is a bra."

Noreen ignored me. She put on a bright pink bra, then slipped her dress over it.

"I hate to break this to you, Noreen, but you look exactly the same with a bra as you did without one."

"I'm not finished." She went to her dresser drawer, pulled out a pair of socks, and stuffed them down the front of her dress. She turned sideways. "How do I look?"

The top of the dress hung loosely over two round little bumps.

"You look like a person with a pair of socks on her chest," I said.

"Wait." Noreen turned back to the dresser drawer and starting packing away more socks. Finally, she turned around. The fabric of the dress stretched snugly across two large breasts.

"Now *that's* impressive," I said. "Toss me some socks. Adulthood, here I come!"

When all my socks were in place, Noreen and I ran down to the bathroom to check out our new equipment. We stood back to back and looked in the mirror. "Are we or are we not eighteen?" Noreen crowed.

"Part of us is definitely eighteen," I said. Then we got laughing so hard, we had to sit on the edge of the bathtub. Finally, we calmed down enough to go back upstairs and start the tattoos.

"Hold still," I said, as I started to draw on her shoulder.

"What are you going to draw?"

"The only thing I'm good at—a horse."

Noreen pulled away. "I don't want horses all over me. That's dumb. Can't you do flowers or something?"

"Not as well as I can do horses. I can do some cartoon characters, though. How about Snoopy or Garfield?"

"Are you kidding? If you do cartoons, they'll know some kid did them. These have to look authentic, so just do your best with the flowers. And throw some hearts in here and there. Tattooed people always have hearts on them."

"Yeah," I said. "With people's names written inside. You want me to write Gino Vivino's name in yours?"

"I can't stand Gino Vivino. Ooh, that tickles."

"If you don't hold still, you're going to have flowers that *look* like horses. How much of ourselves are we going to have covered up with tattoos, anyway?"

"Just what shows with our dresses on. Arms, legs, and faces, I guess."

"We're going to draw on our faces?"

"Sure. It'll be a great disguise. Otherwise somebody might recognize us before the carnival leaves town."

"Do you think our parents will try to find us right away?"

"Sure they will. But remember, it's just because they need us to work for them. We have to hide out long enough to scare them, so they want us back for ourselves." Noreen squirmed in her chair. "This is driving me nuts, Cat. Let's switch for a while, and let me draw on you. Get on the bed. I'll do the backs of your legs."

She was right. It did tickle, especially when she got behind my knees, but I tried hard to hold still. "Are you doing flowers?"

"No, I'm no good at flowers, but this is going to be beautiful. Just wait till I'm finished."

"Let me peek now." I sat up and crossed one leg over the other so I could see the back of my right calf. "What's this skinny orange thing?"

"I told you to wait until I finished."

"But what's it supposed to be?"

"A carrot."

"A carrot!" I switched legs. The other one had little green blobs down the back.

"Those are brussels sprouts," Noreen said proudly.

"You're doing me in *vegetables*?"

"That's what I draw best. I won the Four Basic Food Groups poster contest this year, remember? For the whole county."

"Vegetables are a lot dumber than horses, Noreen. I'm going to look ridiculous."

"Trust me, Cat. It's going to be great. Lie down again so I can finish. We still have to get packed and out of here before people start coming home."

As soon as the last tattoo was finished, Noreen dragged in another carton. "Help yourself to shoes. I'll find the box with the old jewelry."

The shoes were all too big for me, but I found a pair of bright green ones that looked pretty good with my yellow dress. They had real high heels that were as thin as a ball-point pen. Noreen came back with the jewelry box. She had already picked out some long dangling rhinestone earrings for herself.

"I've never seen anybody wear jewelry that fancy in the middle of the day," I said.

"Ordinary people might not, but show biz people do." Noreen had found a pair of purple high heels that almost fit her. Her feet were a lot bigger than mine. She put on the shoes, then twirled around like a model. "What do you think?"

"If I didn't know you, Noreen, I'd swear you were at least eighteen. Maybe even twenty. And you definitely look like show biz."

Noreen grinned. "Here, put these on." She tossed me a raincoat and a hat with a veil.

"What's this stuff for? You won't be able to see our outfits."

"That's the whole idea. We have to keep covered up until we get to the carnival. We don't want anybody in the neighborhood to recognize us. Come on. Help me finish packing."

We shoved two more minidresses into Noreen's backpack, plus an extra pair of high heels and earrings for each of us. Noreen made four peanut butter sandwiches and put in a couple of apples, in case we didn't get paid the first day.

"Shouldn't we leave a note?" I asked.

"Don't be stupid, Cat. We don't want them to know where we're going."

"Not where we're going. Just why we're going."

Noreen handed me a pencil and a piece of paper. "Okay. You do it."

I wrote: "We're tired of getting stuck with all the work. That's why we're running away." We both signed it, but it didn't seem finished, so I added: "P.S. We don't think you love us anymore."

"Nice touch," Noreen said. "That'll get the old guilt rolling."

We left the note on top of a pile of laundry on the dining room table, then walked Noreen's bike over to my house the back way. We were pretty sure nobody would recognize us, but we had to be careful not to be seen, so we stopped at the driveway of the house behind ours. All I had to do was slip along the side of their garage into our yard, then grab my bike and take off.

"Hurry up," Noreen whispered. "I'll just wait here and try to look inconspicuous."

I started along the side of the garage. My high heels kept digging into the soft ground, and the shoes were so loose that one pulled off altogether. As I put it back on, I noticed that the broccoli around my ankles showed below my long black raincoat.

Just as I was about to slip into our garage, our car came into the driveway. I ducked behind the garbage cans and listened as Dad got out of the car. Then I heard Mrs. Lavin, our next-door neighbor, call over the fence to ask how everything was going. At first I felt a little twinge when I heard Dad's voice. I wondered if maybe I was wrong about this running away business. After all, until the babies came along Mom and Dad had always been great. But then, as I listened, I realized that all Dad could talk about were the stupid babies. He and Mrs. Lavin must have gone on for about five minutes, and never once did anybody mention my name. That did it. As soon as Dad went into the house, I slipped into the garage and grabbed my bike.

Noreen hadn't moved a muscle since I left her. "What took you so long, Cat? I was afraid you changed your mind about leaving."

"No way," I said. "Let's go."

As we rode along, I realized why you never see anybody riding a bike in high heels. I had my foot shoved as far into the toe as it would go, so the shoe wouldn't fall off, but the back of it flapped up and hit my heel each time the pedal went around. Noreen's shoes fit better than mine, so she was making better time. It was hard to see through the veil, too. Mine had little black fuzzy dots all over it that looked like spiders dangling in front of my face. I kept forgetting what they were and swatting them.

The light changed just as I got to one corner, and I

had to wait while Noreen got even farther ahead. A little kid and his mother were on the sidewalk with me, waiting for the light to change. "Mommy, look," the kid said, jiggling up and down. "It's Mary Poppins!" His mother pulled him around to the other side of her and whispered something. I thought I heard the words "crazy person."

Chapter Fourteen

We arrived at the carnival grounds just as the afternoon show was letting out. The main tent was huge, with red and green flags fluttering from the tops of the tent poles and all the way down the ropes to the ground. Beyond that was the midway, with game booths and rides. There were about six different kinds of music playing at the same time.

"I wish we had some money," I said. "I'd love to ride the ferris wheel."

"You'll be able to ride on anything you want, as soon as they hire us," Noreen said.

"Free?"

"Sure. It's what they call a fringe benefit. Like in some jobs you get medical insurance and stuff. Here, you get to go on the rides as much as you want."

I didn't know where Noreen got her information, but this was beginning to sound better all the time. "Where do we find Mr. Constantine?"

"We'll have to ask somebody, but first we need someplace to leave our bikes," Noreen said. "We don't want him to know that we didn't drive a car over here. Let's lock them to that chain-link fence." We fastened the bikes securely to the fence and hid the backpack under a nearby bush. I started to take off my raincoat.

"What are you doing?" Noreen said.

"I thought you said we were just wearing the hats and raincoats until we got here."

"Let's leave them on until we find Stavros Constantine. Then we can whip them off and dazzle him. You know—the element of surprise."

I had to admit Noreen thought of all the angles. I buttoned my raincoat back up, and we moved along with the crowd. Most of them were heading for the midway. The afternoon had turned hot, and the crowd was churning up the dust. I was dying to take off the sticky raincoat.

A beautiful black-haired lady stepped out of one of the side entrances to the tent. Her gold costume glittered in the sunlight. "There's somebody who works here," I said. "Let's ask her."

When we got up close, she wasn't so beautiful after all, and her costume was just a faded old orange bathing suit with sequins sewn all over it. "Can you tell us where to find Mr. Constantine?" Noreen asked.

The lady smiled, and I could see that one of her

side teeth was missing. "Which Mr. Constantine you want? This place is crawling with Mr. Constantines."

"Stavros," Noreen said.

The lady looked us over carefully. "Ah, the big boss, you want, eh? Him you'll find in the blue trailer over behind the ten-in-one on the midway."

"What's the ten-in-one?" I asked.

"The freak show. There's a big sign that says Hall of Incredibles. Can't miss it."

"Thanks." Noreen grabbed my arm. "Come on. We'd better find him before the next show starts."

"Are we going to be called freaks, Noreen?"

"No, we're going to be called incredibles. What difference does it make? It's only for a few. . ."

She stopped dead, and when I looked up, I saw why. Coming toward us was a man with a whole bunch of red-headed kids, all carrying cotton candy and stuffed animals. It was Mr. Jablonski and the McNulty clan, and there was no time to dodge them.

"Don't panic," Noreen said, sounding panicky. "Just keep going."

I stared straight ahead and kept walking. Ryan passed so close to me, our shoulders bumped, but he was busy watching the screaming people on the Death Drop, and he never gave us a second look. As soon as they went by, Noreen and I ducked behind a hot dog stand to look back at them.

"That was close," I said.

"Yes, but it worked. Our disguises are so good, even my own brothers don't know who I am. Compared to that, getting hired by the carnival is going to be easy."

The Hall of Incredibles was a long, narrow tent that had a platform running across the front, with huge pictures showing a sword swallower, a fire eater, a man so thin you could see his whole skeleton, a lady with a huge snake wound around her neck, a fat lady, and, sure enough, Dazzling Drinelda, the Tattooed Woman.

In the picture Drinelda was wearing a very skimpy purple bikini, and every inch of her that you could see, except for her face, was covered with designs. She looked as if she were wearing fabric instead of skin. "I told you, Noreen. They already have one. And get a load of those tattoos. You think we can compete with that?" I pushed up my raincoat sleeve and shoved my arm in Noreen's face. Radishes circled my wrist like a bracelet, while a bunch of celery climbed up toward my elbow. "What are they going to call me? Vegetella, the human salad?"

Noreen pushed my arm away. "Shhh. Look!" A huge woman with pale designs all over her body came out on the platform and sat down heavily on a bench in front of Drinelda's picture. "Do you think that's her?"

"How could it be?" I said. "It doesn't look anything like her."

"Well, I think it's her, and she's gotten old and fat, and her tattoos have faded. It should be easy to convince Mr. Constantine that they need a new tattooed woman. Or better yet, two for the price of one."

The sideshow barker stepped up to the microphone. "La-deeeez and gentlemen. You see before you one of the great human wonders of our time. The Dazzling Drinelda, whose body serves as a canvas for over one thousand miniature works of epidermal art created by some of the finest artists in America."

"See? I told you," Noreen said. "It's her. Come on, let's find Mr. Constantine."

"Wait. I want to watch for a minute."

There were some kids hooting at Drinelda, making nasty remarks about how fat she was. She just stared at them and didn't seem to care. Instead of the purple bikini, she was wearing a short pink satin sun dress that was so wide it could have been the skirt from my vanity.

I caught up to Noreen just as she slipped around the side of the tent. "If we take that lady's job away from her, what's she going to do?"

"That's her problem," Noreen said. "We need the job worse than she does."

"But our tattoos aren't even real."

"Maybe hers aren't either. You saw how faded they were. Look. Here it is." Noreen had stopped in front of a blue trailer.

"There's no sign. How do you know this is the right one?"

Noreen rolled her eyes. "Don't be such a wimp, Cat." She knocked on the edge of the screen door.

A tall man with thick black hair and a mustache to match appeared on the other side of the screen. "Yeah?"

"We're looking for Stavros Constantine," Noreen said. Her voice had a little waver in it.

"Who's looking for him?"

Noreen pulled herself up tall. She usually slouched. "We're the Decorative Dancing Dolly Sisters. I'm Florinda, and this is my sister . . . uh, Vegetella."

I moaned inside.

The man stepped down out of the trailer. "I'm Stavros Constantine." He was wearing tight red-satin pants and an undershirt, and he had a rotten-looking unlit cigar tucked behind his ear. He looked from Noreen to me and raised his bushy eyebrows. "You look pretty young to be an act."

"Sure, we *look* young, Mr. Constantine, but we're eighteen," Noreen said.

Mr. Constantine grinned, which made his droopy black mustache stretch into a straight line. "Twins?"

"Naw. I'm nineteen next week. Vegetella here just turned eighteen." She nudged me, and we both whipped off our hats and raincoats. It was all I could do not to yell, *"Ta dah!"* Noreen was right about the element of surprise. Mr. Constantine's mouth fell open, then he broke into an even bigger grin than before, making his mustache turn up at the ends.

"I'm sure you must have heard of us," Noreen continued. "We were real big out in the Midwest. We're the only double dancing tattoo act in the country."

Mr. Constantine stuck the cigar in his mouth and studied my left arm. "Interesting work. I never saw anyone done in vegetables before. Only problem is, I got me a tattooed lady already. Nelda's been with me for twenty-three years. Far as I'm concerned, she's got a job with this carnival for life."

"Couldn't you use a dancing tattoo team, too?" Noreen pleaded. "You'd have the only carnival act with three tattooed ladies. We could be Dazzling Drinelda and the Decorative Dancing Dolly Sisters. You want to see us dance?"

He flipped the cigar to the other corner of his mouth and started to go back into his trailer. "Look, kids. I'd like to give you a break, but I told you . . ."

Noreen was practically crying. "Just give us a chance, Mr. Constantine. Look. We'll show you." She turned to me and whispered, *"Swan Lake!"* Then she started counting. "Three-and-four-and-one."

On "one" she grabbed my arm and took off, humming the Dance of the Four Swans. I'd had enough trouble trying to keep up with her in toe shoes, but in oversize high heels, it was even worse. She looked pretty good, as usual. I, on the other hand, was lurching around like a drunk. I noticed several socks lying on the ground, but I didn't dare check to see which one of us had lost them.

Mr. Constantine leaned up against the trailer and laughed. "*Swan Lake!* One of my favorites." He joined in singing with Noreen, "Dah-dit-dit-dit. Dah-diddle-dit-dit," clapping his hands in time to the music. Noreen and Stavros Constantine were at least three bars ahead of me. By the time we got to the end, I had kicked off my shoes and was dancing in my bare feet. The dust almost completely covered the turnips on the tops of my feet.

"Bravo!" Mr. Constantine shouted, but there was a twinkle in his eyes that made me think he was laughing at us—at me anyway. "Thank you, ladies, for a delightful performance, but I'm afraid the answer is still no. This is no life for two refined girls like yourselves. Best you go home to your family now."

"But we can't," Noreen wailed. "We're orphans. We don't have anybody but each other, and we'll starve if we don't get a job."

Stavros looked over at me, and I knew he was thinking it would be a while before I starved to death.

He glanced at his watch. "You two aren't going to give up easy, are you?" He leaned against the trailer and looked at us for a minute or two. Then he nodded his head, as if he had just made a decision. "Tell you what I'm going to do. It's about time for Nelda to be getting back to her trailer. I think you need to talk to her about your ideas for this new three-tattooed-ladies act. Come on."

He led us through a little back road behind the midway booths. A few of the performers were sitting in lawn chairs outside their trailers. One lady was hanging up a whole row of purple tights on a clothesline that stretched between two trailers. The dog trainers had a big metal tub of soapy water and were hosing off four sudsy poodles. The spicy smell of sausages and peppers from a nearby food stand mingled with the odor of wet dog as we walked past them.

When we got to Nelda's trailer, Mr. Constantine knocked, then stuck his head in the door. "Got a couple of gen-u-wine dancing tattoed ladies want to hook up with your act, Nelda. Call themselves Florinda and Vegetella, the Decorative Dancing Dolly Sisters." He paused, took the cigar out of his mouth, and looked back at us. "Big names in the Midwest," he added, smiling.

A deep husky voice called back. "Send 'em on in, love."

Mr. Constantine bowed and held the door open for

us. Noreen lost her nerve and slipped behind me, shoving me into the dark, stuffy trailer. It was hard to see after being out in the bright sunlight, but I could just barely make out Nelda's shape sitting at a table.

"Have a seat," she said, dabbing at her face with a huge handkerchief. "It's hotter than blazes in here, so I'm having ice tea. Grab a couple of glasses from the cupboard, and I'll pour you some."

I found the glasses and handed them to her. Noreen and I slid into the bench across the table from her. That's when I realized that a large semicircle had been cut out of the table to leave room for Nelda's stomach. It made me think of Mom trying to get into the booth in McDonald's, and I felt a pang of homesickness. I wondered if they missed me yet.

Nelda saw me staring at the hole in the table. She laughed, making the satin dress quiver. "You like my custom-made table? Stavros fixed this for me after I got stuck in here one time and missed the two o'clock show. I hollered like a banshee, but nobody could hear me over the noise of the midway. They had to saw the table right off at the base to get me out."

"Is that really your picture out in front of the tent?" Noreen asked.

"You mean was I ever that skinny, right?"

Noreen bit her lip and nodded.

"That was me, all right. But I always had trouble keeping my weight down so's I could wear those skimpy little costumes. Then one day Stavros and me got the brilliant idea of making me the first tattooed fat lady in history. Stavros had another reason for that. He wanted to be able to fire Tessie. She's about the meanest old fat lady in the business.

"Anyways, there's nothing I don't like to eat, so I started *trying* to gain weight for a change." She laughed, setting off new ripples of pink satin. "Had the best time of my life, until I got to three hundred and sixty pounds. Then I topped out and couldn't gain another ounce no matter how much I ate, so we had to give up on the idea."

Noreen's eyes were huge. "Give up? Isn't that fat enough?"

"Out in the real world it's plenty fat. But to be the official fat lady in a ten-in-one, you gotta be over five hundred. Most of 'em run six and over. Tessie says she's six seventy-five, but she's the worst liar I ever run into. Anyways, compared to her, I'm just pleasingly plump."

My eyes had adjusted to the light now, and I looked more closely at Nelda's tattoos. There were a few fancy birds and things, but most of the pictures were cartoon characters. Batman was on her shoulder, and Superman was flying straight across her chest, his red cape swirling up around her neck. That showed how much Noreen knew, not letting me do Snoopy and Garfield. I elbowed her, but she was already looking. Staring was more like it.

Nelda lifted her arm so we could see the figure of a plump Wonder Woman twirling a golden lasso up into her armpit. "You should have seen these when I was young. The colors was real bright. Just like in the comics. That was my nickname—the Walking Funny Papers. Only trouble is, when I put on weight, my skin stretched out, so they look kind of faded now. Distorted, too. Old Wonder Woman here could stand to go on a diet." She laughed again, and the skin hanging from her arm waggled back and forth like a heavy velvet sleeve.

It was so hot and stuffy in the trailer, my stomach felt queasy. It didn't seem to bother Noreen, though. She drained her glass and set it down on the table. "Mr. Constantine said we could talk about us being a part of your act. Is it okay with you?"

"Depends," Nelda said, looking straight at Noreen. "You think you want to wash those chicken scratches off yourselves and get a set of real tattoos?"

"Real tattoos? But these are . . ."

Nelda reached over to pour Noreen more tea and deliberately spilled some on my arm. Then, before I knew what was happening, she wiped my arm with her handkerchief, smearing my eggplant into a purple streak. Nelda held up the purple-stained handkerchief. "You were saying?"

Noreen slumped back on the bench. "How did you

know our tattoos were fake?"

Nelda grinned. "We get a tattooed lady or two showing up in nearly every town we play. If Stavros can't talk them into going home, he sends them to me. You're the first one with veggies, though."

"I told you it was a corny idea, Noreen," I said. "But would you listen to me?"

"You have to help us, Nelda," Noreen pleaded. "We aren't real sisters, either. I'm Noreen and her name's Cat. We were both treated badly at home, and we can't go back."

Nelda's eyes narrowed. "Your folks beat you?"

"No, not exactly," Noreen said. "But we both have to work all the time, really hard. And our folks don't want us around. They have too many kids anyway."

"So you figure the answer is to run away with the carnival, eh? Nice easy life, you think?"

"We're willing to work hard," Noreen said. "We just want to get paid for it."

Nelda leaned back and put both hands on her stomach. "Sounds reasonable, I guess. Tell you what. I'll fill you in on what carnival life is like, but I'm about half-starved. You two had dinner yet?"

We both shook our heads.

"Fine. You'll eat with me, then." She leaned toward the open window and shouted. "Hey, Cleo, I got me two guests here. Can you bring over a couple extra bowls of that stew?"

A voice yelled back. "Coming right up, Nelda."

"Cleo's the best cook in the carnival. We got a deal. She cooks for me. I sew all her costumes." Nelda reached over and switched on a small TV. "Hope you don't mind, but I like to watch the news while I eat. Only way I can keep up on what's happening in the world. We'll keep it turned low so we can talk, though. Now, about those tattoos. You girls brave enough to get some real ones?"

"What do you mean, brave enough?" Noreen asked.

"Well, it don't tickle, you know. It feels like when you go to the doctor and get a shot—hurts like the devil for a second or two, then stops. Only trouble is, you got to get shot a hundred, maybe hundred fifty times for each tattoo. Then, when the swelling goes down, you got to keep going back for more, until you're covered all over. Nobody's going to pay good money to see one or two tattoos."

I kicked Noreen under the table. She got the message. "Uh . . . maybe we should start out with something else. Is there any other job we could get here?"

Nelda smiled. "Well, Arnold, the sword swallower, is almost ready to retire. You could take his place. That's what I was going to be when I first started out, but I couldn't on account of my allergies."

"You're allergic to swords?" I asked.

"Naw, but the one thing you don't want to do when

you have a sword shoved down your gullet is sneeze. It's do-it-yourself surgery!" She leaned back and laughed. The soft round shapes of her stomach rearranged themselves under the satin. I could feel a few things rearranging themselves in my own stomach.

Just then there was a knock on the door. "Soup's on." A tall, thin woman wearing a gold halter top, a harem skirt, and a thick belt came into the trailer. She set a black pot on the table and got some dishes out of the cupboard.

"This here's my friend Cleo, better know as Cleopatra and Her Serpents of the Nile. Meet...uh... Florinda and Vegetella."

"Pleased to make your acquaintance, I'm sure." As Cleo reached out to shake my hand, I realized her belt was reaching out, too. It was a huge gray snake.

I practically climbed into Noreen's lap, and if the two of us could have squeezed through the small screened window, we would have been out of there.

Nelda patted the snake's head. "No need to be afraid of Howie," she said. "He's an old sweetheart, aren't you, boy?"

Cleo cackled. "Howie wouldn't hurt a fly. He's a little hard on mice, but flies he wouldn't hurt."

The black pot was full of brown goop with shiny little puddles of grease lying on top. As Cleo stirred it up, big chunks of gray meat and vegetables rose to the surface. Cleo had dished up a huge bowl for

Nelda and a smaller one for Noreen, but when she started to dish up mine, Howie's head got in the way. A big blob of glistening gravy dribbled down the snake's neck and plopped into my bowl.

"Oops! Sorry, Howie," Cleo said. She ran her finger up Howie's neck to wipe off the leftover gravy, then popped the finger into her mouth. "Mmmm. Might need a tad more salt."

Everything went kind of blurry for me after that, until I heard Nelda say, "Turn up that TV, Cleo. There's something on about that baby again." My eyes focused on a picture of a baby on the screen. It was Max.

I jumped up and grabbed for the volume knob on the TV, forgetting that I was just inches from a ten-foot snake. "Everybody be quiet. She's talking about my brother!"

Stephanie's voice filled the small trailer. "The smallest of the Corwin quadruplets has taken a turn for the worse. Plagued with respiratory distress syndrome since birth, little Max Corwin was unable to go home with the other three babies earlier this week. Doctors here now feel that Max may not survive the night."

I grabbed Noreen's arm. "We have to go back. Max needs me."

"Hold on a minute," Nelda said. "What are you

talking about, girl? You know that baby?"

I started to cry, but Noreen spoke for me. "She's Cat Corwin. Her mother had quadruplets, and now one of them is real sick. She has to get to the hospital."

"We can take care of that fast enough," Nelda said. She pushed the button on a small box. "Stavros? You there? It's Nelda."

A voice crackled back over the box. "Yeah, Nelda. What's up?"

"Tell the squad car at the front gate to get over here fast. One of these kids is the sister of those quadruplets we've been hearing about on TV. She's got to get to the hospital."

"Okay, Nelda. I'll send them right over."

Noreen and I ran out of the trailer, and Nelda followed, easing herself down the steps. Nelda put her arm around me as we waited for the police. "It's all my fault," I sobbed. "I shouldn't have left."

Nelda hugged me tight, so my face rested on her chest. Superman was smiling at me. "You didn't have a thing to do with what's happening to that baby, Cat. You just get back there so's your Mama don't have two babies to worry about."

I nodded. I could see a flashing red light making its way down the midway.

Nelda rocked me from side to side. "Pretty tough

being the big sister of quadruplets, is it?"

"Yes," I sniffled, and she handed me the big handkerchief.

"It may seem hard now, but there's a lot of good
times in a big family. I should know. I'm the oldest of
nine kids."

"Really?" Noreen said. "I only have five little
brothers."

The police car pulled up, and Noreen and I
climbed in. Nelda ducked down to look in the window. "You two come visit me when we play this town
next year, hear? And bring all your brothers—especially those four babies. We'll go on all the rides. Little Max will love it."

The siren started up, and the crowds parted to let
us through. As we went past the ferris wheel, I tried
to picture Max and me riding it together.

Chapter Fifteen

The police had notified the hospital, so Mom was waiting for us in the lobby. "Thank heaven you're all right. We've been frantic ever since Mrs. McNulty came over to our house with your note." She hugged us both. "The police said they found you at the carnival. What were you thinking of, running away like that? Heaven only knows what might have happened to you. All sorts of strange people hang around at carnivals."

I wriggled out of her hug. "The police didn't find us. One of the carnival people, a very *nice* carnival person, helped us find *them*. We only came back because we heard about Max. Is he all right?"

Mom ran her fingers through her hair. She looked exhausted. "It's still touch and go. The doctors say if he makes it through the night, he probably has a pretty good chance, but he's so little and weak."

"Can I see him?" I asked.

"Yes. Your father is up there now. We just have to be careful not to get in the way of the people who are caring for him, and we can't hold him. He's not..." Mom suddenly looked at Noreen and me as if she were seeing us for the first time. "What on earth do you have all over yourselves? And where did you get those clothes?" Her eyes dropped to my chest. "And where did you get those..." She started to laugh. "Both of you come with me into the ladies' room. And don't think that I'm not mad, just because I'm laughing. I'm furious. This whole thing is definitely not a laughing matter." She giggled again.

Just as we were passing the elevators, the door opened, and Stephanie Bethancourt stepped out, followed by her camera crew. "Well, are these the little runaways? My, don't we look absolutely... ornamental."

I looked past Stephanie and saw my reflection in the mirrored wall next to the elevators. The tomatoes on my cheeks had tear streaks running through them, and tomato juice dribbled down over the onions on my neck.

Stephanie adjusted her earphone and turned to the cameraman. "Let's get a sound level, and we'll do a remote from here. The kid who ran away is back, so we might as well do an update on that, since nothing much is happening upstairs."

Mom held her purse up in front of the camera lens.

"You're not putting this on television, Stephanie."

Stephanie smiled and fluttered her eyelashes. "But Mrs. Corwin, surely you must realize that when you become a public figure, you have to sacrifice a certain amount of your privacy."

Mom went up to Stephanie Bethancourt, looked her straight in the eye, and said, "Stuff it, Steffie." Then she grabbed my arm and Noreen's and dragged us into the ladies' room.

"Boy, you sure told her, Mom," I said.

"Never mind that. We have to get you two looking reasonably presentable. I want you to start by taking out whatever is lurking underneath the tops of those dresses."

Noreen fished out twelve socks, but I could only find five. I must have been leaving a trail of socks ever since *Swan Lake*.

Mom handed me a wet paper towel. "Here. Start scrubbing. You too, Noreen." Mom dampened another towel and handed it to her.

"I bet Ma is really mad, isn't she?" Noreen said.

"She's upset but thankful that you're safe. So's your father. Hurry, because he'll be here to pick you up in a few minutes, and I don't think you want him to see you like this."

"Pa's coming? He never carts us kids around."

"Well, he's coming tonight because your mother is at our house taking care of the babies."

"Really? Why is Mrs. McNulty at our house?" I asked.

"One thing sort of led to another," Mom said, scrubbing at my neck. "Mrs. McNulty came over with the note as soon as she found it, and we decided we should report you missing to the police. Then it wasn't more than ten minutes later that the call came about Max, so she stayed with the babies so I could come here."

Noreen scrubbed frantically at her face and arms. The tattoos didn't all come off, but they mushed into a brownish color, as if Noreen had a real good tan, which seemed funny because all she ever got in the sun were freckles. "I'd better get going, Mrs. Corwin. Pa hates to wait for people."

"All right, Noreen. He should be pulling up by the front entrance. We'll talk more about this at another time."

Noreen hugged me and ran for the door.

"Hey, Noreen. You forgot something," I called.

"What?"

"Your socks."

Dad was in the lounge when we reached Max's floor. "Boy, am I glad to see you." He got up and hugged me so hard I thought my ribs would break.

"What's happening with Max?" Mom asked.

"They're trying to clear out his lungs again, so they asked me to step out. He's fighting, but he seems weaker all the time. I feel so darn helpless."

"When can we go in?" I asked.

"They'll let us know. We might as well sit down and wait."

We all sat down at a little table in the corner of the lounge. "It just wasn't like you to run away like this, Cat," Dad said. "Where have you been? And why did you feel you had to run away instead of talking about it?"

I took a deep breath and plunged in. "Well, nobody had any time to listen to me, and Noreen and I were both sick of having to work all the time. We thought if we just ran away to the carnival for a few days, it would teach you and the McNultys a lesson. So we dressed up to look older and drew tattoos all over ourselves, and we thought Mr. Constantine, the carnival owner, was all set to give us a job. He had us go talk to Nelda, the tattooed lady, in her trailer, and she . . ."

"Her trailer!" Mom interrupted. "You went into a stranger's trailer? Don't you remember anything we taught you about not going into a person's house if you don't know them?"

"I . . . I'm sorry, Mom. Being all dressed up and trying to get a job like that, I guess we didn't feel like kids anymore. The old rules didn't seem to matter."

"Well, you *are* kids, and the rules definitely matter!" Mom said, her voice going up a notch. "You and Noreen were incredibly lucky that the people you ran into could be trusted. Don't you ever do anything like this again, do you hear?"

Dad had been sitting there breaking little pieces off a Styrofoam cup. "I don't know what to say, Cat. Running away was wrong. I'm sure you know that. But if we made you feel we'd stopped loving you because of the babies, then your mother and I are at fault, too."

Mom looked like she was going to keep yelling at me. Then she took a deep breath and slumped back in her chair. "I guess you have a point, Walter." She reached over and took my hand. "That fight we had was awful, Cat. We both said things we didn't mean."

"I know. I only yelled those things at you because I was so mad and tired. Everything was crazy with the babies crying all the time."

"Crazy isn't the word for it," Mom said. "I wish we'd had Mrs. McNulty over the minute the babies came home. I never realized what a wonder she is with infants. She felt terrible about Noreen, too. She's always given Noreen more than her share of work because she's so much more dependable than the boys, but she never realized how much Noreen resented it."

Dad pulled an envelope out of his pocket. "Speaking of Noreen, I finally opened the envelope from that dance teacher of yours."

He handed it to me.

Dear Mr. and Mrs. Corwin:

I was delighted to hear of the birth of your quadruplets. I'm sure you have incurred many extra expenses during this period, and I hope you won't be offended if I award a full scholarship to Catherine for the coming year, starting with the summer session.

This is my way of offering my congratulations to you, and my thanks to Catherine for the fine effort she has put forth this year.

Sincerely yours,
Yvette Girardeau

"A scholarship! That's wonderful!"

"That's not all," Dad said. "We have a surprise for you." He pulled a folded piece of paper from another pocket and smoothed it out on the table in front of me. There was some sort of floor plan drawn on it in pencil. "I'm not much of an artist, so I'll have to explain this to you. Your new room has a pretty-good sized closet. I'm going to tear it out and build you a loft bed, with built-in drawers beneath and a cupboard for hanging clothes on one side, a desk on the other. You see, with all the furniture packed into the closet, the room itself can be a dance studio. I'll put a barre along this wall, and you can put your mirrors over here. Eventually, we can do the whole wall in mirror tiles."

I turned the paper over. It was a McDonald's placemat.

Mom smiled. "We felt awful about having to take your room for the babies. Your father sketched this one night when we went to McDonald's. You went out to the car ahead of us, remember?"

I remembered, all right. While I was out in the car crying because Mom and Dad didn't care about me anymore, they were planning this. I couldn't say anything.

Dad shrugged and started to fold up the paper. "Of course it's not as big as your old studio, but . . ."

"Dad, it's perfect. I love it. I just never knew. . ."

Just then Dr. Braxton came in. Mom jumped up from the table. "How is Max doing?"

"Not well, I'm afraid, Diane. You can all go in now, but please don't try to touch him, and if he goes into any sort of crisis, you must leave immediately. I know that sounds harsh, but everything is a life-and-death battle with Max at this point."

"We understand," Mom said, her mouth set in a grim line.

Even though we weren't going to be able to touch

Max, we still had to scrub our hands with the special soap and put on masks and gowns. Max wasn't in the isolette anymore. He was in an open crib with a lamp over it. There seemed to be more wires and tubes attached to him than ever before.

"Why is he in a different bed?" I asked.

"The lamp gives off heat," Dad said. "They're just trying to make sure he stays warm."

Max looked so helpless. Each breath seemed to use up all of his strength, and his throat caved in every time he struggled to take in more air.

"Hang on, little guy," Dad whispered. "You have your big sister out here rooting for you now." He pulled me close to him.

I kept listening to the beep of the heart monitor, knowing that as long as it kept going, Max was okay. The three of us stood together for a long time, not saying anything, just trying to give Max our strength. The monitor chirped away the minutes in the background.

Then suddenly the beeping stopped, and a high-pitched alarm went off. Nurses and doctors seemed to appear out of nowhere. One of the nurses pushed us toward the door as the loudspeaker said, "Dr. Braxton, call E-4. Dr. Braxton, call E-4." We had to flatten ourselves against the wall as two men in blue shot past us.

Dad led Mom and me across the hall, and we huddled together while we watched through the glass wall of the nursery. The alarm had stopped, and Max was completely surrounded by doctors and nurses, so all we could see was a mass of blue backs. Dr. Braxton ran right by us but didn't say anything. I saw one nurse put a shot into a tube that hung over Max's crib. Then, one by one, the people started moving away, until only Dr. Braxton and one nurse were still with Max. The other nurses and doctors left in twos and threes. Nobody looked at us.

"Is Max okay now?" I asked.

Mom didn't say anything, but I could feel her grip tighten on my shoulder as Dr. Braxton came toward us.

The doctor rubbed his hand over his forehead, then looked up. He put his hands on Mom's shoulders. When I looked up, I could see tears in his eyes. "I'm sorry, Diane. I thought we could pull him through. I really did."

Mom pulled herself taller and took a deep shaky breath. "May we see him?"

"Of course. Do you want me to stay with Cat while you two go in?"

"It's up to her." Mom looked at me. "Do you want to see Max one last time, Cat?"

"What happened?" I asked. "Did Max die?"

Mom nodded.

It had all happened so fast, I didn't know what to

say. I was scared because I'd never seen a dead person before, but I had to say good-bye to Max. "Yes," I whispered. "I think I want to."

A nurse had disconnected the tubes and was starting to untape the wires on Max's chest when we went into the nursery. Mom pushed her hand away. "I'd like to do that," she said quietly. I stood half behind Dad, clinging to his belt, as Mom gently untaped all of the wires. Then she took the little blue hat off and smoothed his hair. Max had the same blond fuzz as the others.

"For the first time in his life, he looks peaceful," Dad said.

He did. Max looked as if he were sleeping, and he almost had a little smile on his face. He was beautiful.

The nurse was standing a short distance away. Mom turned to her. "Is there someplace we could go to be alone with Max for a few minutes?"

"Certainly. There's a private lounge through that door. Just let me know if you need anything."

Mom took a little blue blanket off the pile on a cart, carefully wrapped Max in it, and picked him up. He looked just the way the other three had the day we took them home. We followed her into the next room and sat down on a couch, with Mom and Max in the middle.

Mom raised Max up in her arms and rested her cheek on his. Then she let him slowly back down to her lap. "Such a short life," she said softly.

Dad put his arm around Mom and looked at Max. He ran his finger under Max's chin and started to say something, but all that came out was a choked sob. Then he squeezed his eyes tight and began to cry. I'd never seen Dad do that before. Mom leaned her head against Dad's shoulder and her tears came, too. She pulled me close to her with her free arm. At that moment, I loved Mom and Dad more than I ever had in my whole life.

I looked down into Max's little face. "Good-bye, Max," I whispered. "You'll always be my favorite brother."

Chapter Sixteen

Max's funeral was two weeks ago. Both sets of my grandparents, my aunt and uncle, and three cousins flew in from California. I didn't really remember any of them because we hadn't seen them since I was four, but I liked them all, and I think they liked me, too. Grandma Corwin said it's a crime that families only get together for funerals and weddings. She's going to send me an airplane ticket so I can go visit her and Grandpa Corwin next summer—an airplane trip across the whole country all by myself. I can't wait! I'll have to make sure I'm not away when Nelda is in town with the carnival, though. Dad says when the babies get a little older, we'll drive out to California.

I was just thinking, only a few months ago our family was Mom, Dad, and me. Now we have the babies, and Purrson and her kittens, and I have a whole bunch of relatives who are real people to me now, instead of just names on Christmas presents. It's funny how things can change so fast.

We finished supper a few minutes ago, and I'm sitting here in the middle of the living room floor with all three babies in their infant seats watching the kittens chasing a wad of paper around. Purrson is curled up in the corner, keeping one eye on her babies.

Tim, Seth, and Ian don't cry as much anymore. The day Mrs. McNulty took care of them, she figured out that they stayed a lot happier if they could see each other. Some days they can keep each other entertained for almost an hour at a time. We've even pushed their cribs together so they can see each other as they fall asleep. Of course, they still act like beasts part of the time, but when that happens, we just pile them into the car and drive around the block a few times, like before.

They're growing fast now. Seth is chubby, and Ian is getting long, with the biggest feet I ever saw on a baby. Dad says he'll probably be a basketball player. Tim is the quietest one, but he notices more things than the others and likes to play with his own fingers. We aren't dressing them alike, because Mom says each baby should be his own person.

Summer session has started at Madame Yvette's, and I'm having a great time, even though Wella Mae Riddle is back. She's out of the cast now, but she still has to wear a sling in dance class. She had her mother

PICK OF THE LITTER 151

make her a different-color sling to match each leotard. Is that sickening, or what? She's playing the
broken arm bit for all it's worth. Wella Mae Riddle is
a major pain.

Dad has almost finished my new room, except for
the desk. But since it's summer, I don't have home-
work anyway. Noreen and I love to sit up on my bed
and talk. It feels like being in a treehouse, and Noreen says it'll be a great hideout when the babies get
old enough to be pests. Noreen is practically an ex-
pert on pests. She should be coming over any minute
now because she only has to do the supper dishes
every fifth night. She rotates with all of her brothers
except Patrick, and tonight is Ryan's turn. The boys
are helping to baby-sit Patrick part of the time, too.
They're teaching him how to play football, and he
loves to tackle. Now he tackles people even when he
isn't playing football. The mailman got real mad at
Patrick a couple of days ago.

We all miss Max. Sometimes I'll start thinking
about him all of a sudden, and I can't help crying.
That happens to Mom and Dad, too. But when it
does, we hug each other real hard until it doesn't hurt
quite as much anymore. I think a lot about what it
would have been like if Max hadn't died. It makes me
sad to know that he'll never have the chance to go on
the midway rides with Nelda, or drink Mom's hot
chocolate with tons of marshmallows, or smell the air

after a thunderstorm. He must have known he was going to miss out on a lot of good stuff, because he tried so hard to stay alive. There were so many things I could have taught him. But I guess Tim, Seth, and Ian will need teaching too.

Ian giggled right out loud just now, because he was wiggling his toes, and the gray kitten pounced on them. Mom still isn't letting me keep all of the kittens, but she did say I could pick out one of them. Mrs. McNulty says they'll take the other two, so it's not like I'll never see them again. We're keeping Purrson, of course, but she's going to have an operation so she won't keep having babies.

The kittens are all so cute, I'm having a hard time making up my mind. I wonder which kitten Max would have chosen? I felt kind of funny about that at first because I had promised him the pick of the litter. But I don't think Max would mind. I just hope that wherever Max is now, he can have all the kittens he wants.

ABOUT THE AUTHOR

MARY JANE AUCH is the author of several books for young readers. Her first novel, *Cry Uncle!*, also published by Bantam Skylark Books, was awarded the 1986 work-in-progress grant by the Society of Children's Book Writers. *Pick of the Litter*, her second novel, has been nominated for several state awards.

A free-lance writer and illustrator, the author also works part-time as a writing teacher and library volunteer. Mary Jane Auch lives with her husband and two grown children on a small farm near Rochester, New York. She has never had quadruplets.

Rock 'n roll...
Fun in Puerto Rico...
and summer vacation!

You'll love these great Skylark books—
order them all!